Ghosts
A Short Story Anthology

Edited by

Lana Polansky and Brendan Keogh

Copyright © 2013 by Lana Polansky

All rights reserved. Without limiting the rights under copyright reserved above, no part of this publication may be reproduced, stored in or introduced into a retrieval system, or transmitted, in any form, or by any means (electronic, mechanical, photocopying, recording, or otherwise) without the prior written permission of the copyright owner of this book.

Ghosts in the Machine is a work of fiction. The names, characters, places, and events are either products of the author's imagination or are used fictitiously, and any resemblance to actual persons, living or deceased, business establishments, events, locales is entirely coincidental.

ISBN: 978-1-304-27044-3

Front and back cover design credit: Max Temkin, creator of tabletop game, Cards Against Humanity. Find him on Twitter @MaxTemkin and check out his blog and portfolio at http://maxistentialism.com/.

TABLE OF CONTENTS

Preface—Lana Polansky..4

GDD—Ashton Raze...6

March 2010—Denis Farr..15

Unto Dust—Maddy Myers..19

Ten Steps—Lana Polansky..28

All Time Heroes—Matt Riche...35

The Hierarchy of Needs—Ian Miles Cheong..................................44

Slow Leak—Rollin Bishop..47

If the Sun Rises Again—Dylan Sabin..51

A Perfect Apple—Alois Wittwer...61

See You on the Other Side—Shelley Du.......................................69

Patched Up—Ryan Morning..81

Supercollider—Alan Williamson...92

Good Losers Are Pretty—Andrew Vanden Bossche......................99

Who We Are...108

Preface
Lana Polansky

One summer, I worked at a videogame testing facility as a "functionality" tester. It was my job to find and report all product malfunctions, big and small.

I can't go into much explicit detail about what I saw or did—I'm bound, to this day, by a big, scary non-disclosure agreement to keep my mouth shut. But while I was there, I found endless amusement and stimulation in all the myriad ways a game world could break down, not work, or be incomplete. In many cases, I found myself wondering if I wouldn't find the game more interesting if the bugs were left in.

Screenshots and animated gifs of bugs in popular games (often of the open-world variety) tend to fetch a high value in terms of social currency. These clipping and collision and AI mishaps stand out because, after all, a game is something many of us have come to expect to be a polished product. We find these bugs comical or surreal or, in some cases, genuinely upsetting. These snapshots of mistakes and oversights often compel, even if only as curiosities. And this says nothing of all those conceptual idiosyncrasies and peculiarities that we take for granted, not because they're logical or sensible but because they don't halt the player's momentum.

Games like GZ Storm's *Vidiot Game*, for example, or those by Michael Brough (*Corrypt, Zaga-33*) or thecatamites (*Goblet Grotto, Space Funeral*), will take things a step further, making exploits, bugs and idiosyncrasies into self-conscious parts of the play experience. Instead of being discarded as deficiencies that break the fantasy, they get incorporated into the relationship between the player and the game; they inform the worlds we inhabit, and they in many cases become the stewards of theme and symbolism that make these games more relevant to the people playing them.

Then there's the work of photographer Robert Overweg, whose snapshots of glitches in virtual worlds are an embodiment of Susan Sontag's observation in *On Photography* that "To photograph is to appropriate the thing photographed." Overweg's photos of functionally annoying or visually jarring bugs are evocative, suggestive, almost totally decontextualized from the "polished" games they belong to. A house simply missing texture to a gamer is a symbol of dilapidation and despair to the viewer of a well-angled screenshot.

Ghosts in the Machine was put together with this outlook in mind. These stories aren't meant as fanfiction (though many of us, including myself, have written our share of fanfiction and hold nothing against it). While the stories do draw inspiration from those games that have been so formative to their writers, they are each original works drawing from a specific videogame "problem"— maybe one that takes us out of the fantasy, maybe one that's protected by the fantasy that we've learned not to question.

It might be tempting to ask why we didn't just make a game. But I think the better question is, "What is the difference between prose fiction and videogames?" It's been repeated many times—by Darius Kazemi, by Merritt Kopas, by Richard Lemarchand and many others—that games do what they do best by inviting players to explore systems. But prose—and for that matter, the short story—explore ideas largely through causal relationships. Time, space and perspective are accounted for differently. An entire tale can be told through monologue alone. The same assumptions that we make when we suspend disbelief for a videogame can't necessarily be made when we're reading fiction. This is what excites me about exploring the formal and conceptual pitfalls of one form through the lens of another.

I worked at a facility that ran on the principle of videogame flaws as undesirable. Of course, games, like stories, need editors. Games need to be playable in order to communicate, just like stories need to be readable. But the mistakes and peculiarities of games can also speak for their creators, as flaws have a habit of being revealing of the attitudes and conditions that led to them being there. The stories in this anthology were written by a superb group of contributors—some of whom are veteran writers, some of whom are visual artists, some of whom make games themselves— and co-edited by *Killing is Harmless* author Brendan Keogh (to whom I offer endless thanks) and myself. We believe these stories demonstrate why the things that can go wrong in videogames can also be treated as significant and humanizing in their own right, and we're proud to share them with you.

GDD

Ashton Raze

[All good games start with a great idea.]

If I had my own game, if I could make games or think up worlds or had any fucking imagination whatsoever, this wouldn't be a problem. Type type type, a few lines of code, head onto Twitter, find an artist or two, find a guy to lay down the beats *[a good soundtrack will immerse players in your game]* put it all together. No more of this drivel, control wrenched from me, switching to autopilot, watch as the scene unfolds. Orchestral swells score dragon swoops, string crescendo, clash and clang of steel *[high quality sound effects can really add to the feel]* and yawn through another cutscene.

If I had my own game, I'd play it.

I can do it, they say; they all say I can. This bitter fucking no-hoper without an original idea *[keep a design diary; note down any ideas you have before you forget them]* could do it. Instead, instead of sitting, languishing, controller clenched in tense grip, vice-like, *[be sure not to frustrate the player—test your game thoroughly]* cursing as I clip through the wall, my companion flails in tree roots. Or maybe it's a racer, the damage model's off, these fuckers know nothing about track design. Or a shooter, brazenly all-American *[gunshot puncturing silence and a fistbump for solidarity can go a long way]* filled with cursing and lazily-drawn blood decals. Did the QA monkeys even bother to test this bit?

If I had my own game, I'd test the shit out of it.

But what chance do I have? Can't code, can't think, can't even hold down a steady job. Working afternoons at the bookstore, scowling over a copy of *250 Indie Games You Must Play*. Final warning, but not for that. If I could just *[sort out a self-employment tax reference number]* work harder and maybe just pin something down, turn this whole 'playing videogames' thing into more than just a pastime, I know I could make it. All this turgid shite, all these frustrations, I know I could do a better job. Then, when I put my game out there, let's see all those shill reviewers make asses of themselves by giving it a bad score. This is another problem *[perhaps consider a loan if you need to get your development studio off the ground]* because I don't have the money to pay off the big sites like some of those publishers obviously do. And some of the indies too, obviously. I mean, a 7/10 for a fucking feminist visual novel? 10/10 for a buggy, broken open world RPG? Come on. That's not what gamers want. Reviewers are so out of touch with modern gaming, *[an 8-bit platformer or a SNES-era JRPG is always a good place to start]* it's not even funny.

Flash. Flash is good. Flash games on Newgrounds or Kongregate. You get some good shit on there, and the creators are sometimes barely literate. If they can do it I can do it. This quest is broken, though. How does stuff like this even get released? What kind of piece of shit do you have to be to rip off customers like this? Makes me so mad.

***

I'm at work. I'm not reading that indie game book, that was ages ago, don't take my anecdotes literally. I've been scribbling on a pad, desperately trying to crowbar inspiration out of my brain *[take care in choosing your engine—remember, you may be stuck with it for the duration of your project]* and onto the page. So far I've got a level with spikes and a little dude who has to leap over them. It's a bit like that one game, but not bullshit hard like that, and not made by a couple of *[an original hook is holding down a button to affect gravity]* clowns who never played a platformer in their lives. I'm at work, and this girl approaches me. Great body, smooth-as-hell legs, but she's wearing a jumper and I can't see as much of her torso as I'd like. Not bad, though. The only real perk to working in a bookshop is being able to check out hot nerdy girls, and most of them aren't faking it if they're actually in here buying Sartre or whatever.

She comes up to me at the desk and I'm still doodling in my notepad. I've written down B = 8/F = 6. Body, face. I make no attempt to cover it up, not like she'll know what it means. I am disconnected.

"Do you have any copies of *The Secret History*?" she asks, "Because I really need a copy for college." And I ask her if she's tried checking the shelves and she's like, "that's the thing, I can't remember who wrote it."

She glances down at my notepad, back up at me. I smile, avoiding her gaze, my eyes drifting down to her chest instead. If she notices, she doesn't let on. I tap away at the computer, look it up,

7

find *[be sure to play similar games in your chosen genre—learn from the successes, and the failures]* the author (Donna Tartt), we have two copies in stock I tell her. "Thanks," she says, then waits.

"Can I help you with anything else?" I say, while resuming my doodling. There's a bottomless pit now, and at the bottom is a bunch more spikes. Wait, no, it's not bottomless then, is it? There's a silence, a bottomless pit in the conversation, perhaps that's where I got it from.

"Who wrote it then?" she asks. I don't like her tone. "I need to know where to look." I sigh, and go straight to the correct shelf, grab the book, come back. I hand it to her.

"Did they make a movie of this or am I thinking of something else?"

"No, they didn't, you moron," I want to say, but don't, or, "My own fucking generation makes me sick. Movie version? Just read the damn book," I want to say, but don't. Instead I tell her no, because if they had it'd be one of those shitty movie tie-in editions and it isn't *[the best way to ensure there is no disconnect between player agency and your narrative is to script your game in a dynamic way]* and she seems resigned and accepting about this. She pays by card, and I see her name is Carla. I watch her as she leaves. She has quite a nice ass.

***

Later, I leave work and go home. Dishes fill the sink, my lazy shit of a roommate no doubt too busy fucking his girlfriend to bother to clean up after himself. Or were they mine? I don't recall, because I think *[adding cooperative play to your platformer can transform it into a best-selling title]* mine are still in my room.

I sit at the computer and the internet is bullshit. I play some Flash games, and they're all bullshit. I rate a few, leave a few comments. I'm already picturing my game up there, top of the rankings, a game for gamers by a gamer. None of this corporate-funded red-tape crap. I have the freedom to create the type of game I'd like to play. I go back to playing games on my console, carry on with my archer build, but it all feels so asinine now. I think about that girl Carla a bit and feel a bit guilty for being snappy. Maybe she just likes movies. It's hardly a crime. *[It's important for your central character to have a motive. A girlfriend, kidnapped, who he has to rescue, is a good motivator. Or perhaps she's not his girlfriend, at least not yet, and he wins her over with his daring rescue. Maybe he could be a knight, an agile knight.]*

Talking of movies, I torrent a movie, the inspirational one. The one with Blow and Fish and those guys I mentioned earlier. It's alright, and I think, one day this could be me. Loads of them started out making Flash games. Mostly I don't really care, but Blow says something that resonates with me, something about taking his deepest flaws and vulnerabilities and putting them in the game *[eliciting emotion from the player is definitely something to think about]* and I am down with that. That's how you make a meaningful experience. That's what these big budget games are lacking; the human touch. They're churned out by corporations, there's no soul, and increasingly these days they're pandering to the limp-dicked faggot liberal brigade but *[consider porting your game to a wide variety of formats, in particular mobile platforms]* with indie games, with MY game, I can make what I want to make, say what I want to say, and nobody can stop me or argue otherwise. It is my right, my god-given right, my right to freedom of speech. I am an artist, *[never compromise]* a creator, and I'm beginning to understand how to do this now.

If I made a game, it would represent me: the gamer, the person, the man. Playing the game would be like seeing the world through my eyes.

Somewhere in the distance, a dog barks. I laugh at the irony of the situation when I'm trying to be deep. I can hear my roommate, and my roommate's girlfriend. My roommate is called Danny and I met him through Craigslist looking for a house share, and he's cool I guess *[do not be concerned about making a game to please everyone, it is a fool's errand]*. Plays some games, doesn't hassle me, but his girlfriend really is a total bitch. I won't even go into specifics but seriously, some people fucking astound me with their rudeness and shit.

Later still, I am sitting at the kitchen table eating a bowl of cereal. I normally eat in my room, but I wanted to use the table. I'm making notes. My little dude, Sir *[players want to feel like the hero. Give your character a strong, masculine jaw and a clear sense of justice]* Brian is leaping, tumbling, swinging *[a rope swing mechanic will add a retro feel, igniting memories of* Pitfall*]* and saving his princess. I think about possible metaphors but decide to keep it simple. Danny's girlfriend wanders into the kitchen. She's wearing a bathrobe and when she stands at the fridge I can see her left breast just through the opening in her robe. She sees me and smiles.

"Hey, Chris."

"Hi," I mutter.

She closes the fridge and comes over with a carton of orange juice—MY orange juice—and sits down. "Whatcha doin'?"

"I am designing a game," I say, looking down at my game design document, trying to highlight the obvious.

She laughs, and I know there's scorn implied. "Really? Didn't know you could code."

What the fuck does she know about coding? Her robe's too small for her and I can still see her tits [*RPG elements, if implemented right, can work cross-genre*] a bit. I don't care if she sees me looking; she's a bitch.

"I can't, yet," I say. "Working on it."

"Well, good luck," she says. Doesn't even bother to ask what kind of game it is.

"Hey, while you're here, have you got any idea when you'll be able to give Danny your rent check?" [*It's important to ensure that the player is engaged at all times*]. Oh, here it is. Here she goes again. Sick of her already.

"Soon," I mutter, and gather up my notes. There goes my train of fucking thought.

***

Four months later and I still can't code. I still can't make my game.

It feels like forever since I started. I am making next to no progress. That's a lie, actually. I've made a lot, just not in the right directions. I have pages and pages and pages of notes [*meticulously planning your game will pay dividends in the long run*] and I know pretty much exactly what I want my game to be like. But I was bad and got distracted, life got in the way, and everything's fallen apart.

Carla came back to the store. It was about a month before I lost my job. I'd finished playing that RPG and moved onto a multiplayer shooter phase. 60 hours clocked and speechless at the idiotic fucking design flaws the developers had left in. It's like they've never played a game before [*if you are making a game, acting on player feedback is important*]. Carla came back a bunch of times, actually, and it turns out she'd never noticed my rudeness, I guess, or never cared. We ended up becoming friends, and then got closer. We nearly hooked up, or so I thought, but I told her how I felt about her and things went a bit wrong, which is honestly a relief because I was done with her. I refuse to be friendzoned. All girls are the same. You say one thing wrong, just do one wrong thing, after being the nicest fucking guy *[do not punish the player excessively—while extreme difficulty can work, it is a delicate balance that often requires years of developmental practice]* and you're no longer good enough. Maybe if I'd treated her like shit or whatever she'd have liked me, I dunno. I expended so much energy on this girl, tried to do fucking everything for her, but no, she was interested in some guy who by all accounts is a massive douche which is fairly typical *[creating a believable antagonist, the perfect foil for your main character, is the key to a strong narrative]* I guess. All that time, energy and emotion wasted, and no further progress on games development. What did I get out of it by the end? Nothing. Fucking nothing. A broken heart, a wasted few months *[your player's time is precious. Every aspect of the game should serve a purpose]*, and not even a sympathy fuck.

All that time, up until now, those words resonated through my mind. Blow's words, those softly-spoken syllables dancing in the back of my head. Take your deepest flaws and vulnerabilities. Put them in the game. *[Take your deepest flaws and vulnerabilities. Put them in the game]*.

Fuck you, Jon Blow. Fuck you, you coward. I've played your stupid fucking game, with its metaphor and allegory and what-the-fuck-ever. It's just Mario in a business suit. I've played it, I've played your deepest flaws and vulnerabilities. And so what? Your deepest flaws are time travel and jumping? Or if it's more, why keep them hidden? Why mask them in colorful design and cutesy characters? *[A player will look for reflections of a game's author. Be sure they see you the way you want to be seen]*. It's not that, not just that. Take everything. Your highs, your lows, every fucking aspect of your character and put them in the motherfucking game. Become your game. You are your game. You live, breathe, eat, sleep, die by your game. Fuck your flaws and vulnerabilities. I will use my everything.

It's easy when you know how. It's easy to work it out, easy to undo your best laid plans, easy to overhear your roommate *[be sure to enlist some trusted beta testers]* Danny talking with his girlfriend about when they're going on vacation. Easy to set up auto-emails on a timer, easy to *[remember your early builds may contain bugs]* go to the mall and buy the knife, the cables, the plastic sheeting. It's easy *[act on any feedback, talk to your players]* but it hurts. Suffer for your art. Become the game you want to make. Pour your heart and soul into it. You are not a faceless corporation. *[You are not a faceless corporation.]*

If I had my own game, it would be a reflection of myself.

Here I sit, suspended, gouges red and bloody, my essence, everything, flowing into the machine, replacing my need for knowledge or skill. It is *[i am disconnected]* draining me, sucking me dry, I am becoming the game. By a gamer, for the gamers, you will play *[i am in beta]* my very soul and you will fucking like it. Cables spill from my *[i am golden]* throat as I narrate; tears pour from my eyes as the pain begins to throb. Just me, opening my heart to the world. Each cut a level, each twist a hurdle to overcome. I laugh *[announcement incoming]* and blood bubbles into my throat, over my lips.

Play me, you fucks.

[For your initial release, self-sacrifice is not advised. Test out the technique on an animal or loved one before committing yourself to code.]

***

Text: Review of Super Knight Leaper for GameRanx, written by Ashton Raze. Dated April 19th, 2013.
Used with permission.

Review: Super Knight Leaper
by Ashton Raze

Developer: Christopher B. Broake
Format: Windows (version tested), Mac
Released: Out now (Steam, Desura)
Price: $4.99

Indie platformers are a dime a dozen these days, with the excellent *Super Meat Boy* leading the pack when it comes to arcade action, and the recent *Thomas Was Alone* sitting alongside *Braid* and *Limbo* if you're after a more narrative-driven experience. To stand out from the crowd, you really have to do something special. The much-anticipated *Super Knight Leaper*, despite its generic name, certainly leaps for the stars.

Unfortunately, its jump falls significantly short, and the result is a painful faceplant of epic proportions. Despite the pre-release hype, *Super Knight Leaper* is an unfinished, unenjoyable disaster. With any debut release from an unknown developer, certain flaws can be forgiven, but here...

Honestly I don't know where to start. The game's a mess. From the generic opening level in which Sir Brian's girlfriend is kidnapped (complete with painful chiptune renditions of classic Skrillex tracks), to the horrific collision detection, the sloppy, incomprehensible art and the pitiful dialogue.

Sir Brian struggles to make even the simplest of jumps, and in a game about leaping over spikes, this is a significant problem. Holding down the up arrow allows you to sort of...float around, but occasionally, and without warning, gravity will send you plummeting down to earth and often to an untimely death. Every so often, if you brush up against a wall, the character sprite will begin to vibrate, and eventually the level will reset. Bug? Deliberate mechanic? Who knows. Nothing about Super Knight Leaper makes much sense.

Even more confusing is the narrative, which seemingly has nothing to do with the disastrous events unfolding on screen. The voice acting is delivered in an angry whisper, and is comprised of little more than guttural sounds with the odd curse word thrown in. Occasionally, text appears on the screen, although this does not match what's being said, and seems to be a series of quotes from other, more successful games and—in one particularly unusual instance—from the GameSpot review of *Skyrim*.

Why do these things happen? This is a question you'll give up asking long before you stop questioning why you wasted five dollars on this game. If you do persevere, which I do not advise, you'll be met with a few sections towards the end that could almost be described as genius if they appeared in a better, remotely playable platformer. The penultimate boss, for instance, is Edmund

McMillen's head, but beating it seems to require more luck than skill. I'm still not entirely sure if I ended up winning the battle, or just glitching my way to the next level. Then, at the end, after a painfully bad, hour-long section, you finally reach your princess. Perhaps attempting to mimic *Braid*, or even *Super Mario Bros.* in ending with some kind of twist, your princess turns towards the screen, staring, and points silently, her face emotive. The scene freezes. Ten minutes later, the game closes. No end credits, no game over, just… a quit to desktop.

It's unfathomable how this even got released, let alone how the developer is daring to charge money for it. Save your cash. Buy something—anything—else. Hell, with the time you'd spend playing *Super Knight Leaper*, you'd be better off learning how to develop your own game. Just make sure you use this as a reference guide of what not to do, ever.

A broken, muddled mess of a game that will leave you wishing you'd saved your money. Perhaps worth a look as a bizarre curio, an example of when the hype train gets it wrong, but nothing more.
Score: 2/10

***

Text: Review of Super Knight Leaper for GameRanx, written by Ian Miles Cheong. Dated July 7th, 2013.
Used with permission.

News: Super Knight Lawsuit
by Ian Miles Cheong

The strange case of *Super Knight Leaper* took an even more bizarre turn today as, after a failed petition, thousands of gamers have filed a lawsuit against the game's elusive creator. Reminiscent of 2012's "Retake *Mass Effect*" campaign, the lawsuit was brought about after hundreds of forum users discovered the software was causing slow, yet widespread file corruption. Attempts to identify and combat the virus have thus far met with failure. If successful, the lawsuit could cost the developer of *Super Knight Leaper* in excess of ten million dollars. The game's mastermind, Christopher B. Broake, could not be reached for comment.

March 2010
Denis Farr

PAGE 1

This close.

This close, his face doesn't seem nearly as impressive—no longer crowned with the might to plague your every move, and to send you through days of tortuous ritual and frustration. Your hand runs through his hair, grasping it tightly as you pull him within inches of your own face.

He's kneeling, yanked off the ground slightly by your pull. Already a hollow symbol of anything he was.

Here is the man who destroyed your life. Your husband? A pile of ashes, all because of this pile of filth's actions. He watched outside as your love was caught, screaming, in the house surrounded by soldiers. The life you once led, instead conscripted to deal with the problems he created.

You became a pawn. Whether or not fate guided him, he stood firmly in your path. He set the motions into place. He dies.

Focused. All that is visible anymore is his face, your right hand clenched in his hair, and your left hand gnarled into a fist, looming over you both. He's beaten. You've won.

—*Pull back your face and go in with the fist, go to* **PAGE 2**.
—*Pull his nose to yours, glaring into his eyes, go to* **PAGE 6**.

PAGE 2

With a clumsy precision, you snap back your face as your fist connects with his cheek. There is a resounding thump—a sound like a steak being slapped onto a cutting board sound. Before you can fully process what you will do next, your fist has snapped back and is driving toward his face again.

He utters some unintelligible sound. Pain speaks a much clearer and more concise message than any language at his disposal. As does blood, which starts trickling out of his mouth by the time your third punch hits.

There is a terrified keen coming from him as you pause for a moment.

Looking at him now, it's difficult to imagine he was ever a threat to you. How could this ruin of a man have ever come into your life and wrecked it so thoroughly? You once again shove his face into yours. At first it slips a bit, before you hover it just slightly from the tip of your nose.

This close?

This close, all you really see anymore is red.

—*Continue the assault, go to* **PAGE 4**.
—*Pause ana stare, go to* **PAGE 6**.

PAGE 3

You can't do this, can you? Can you really push yourself so far? Then again, you've already killed plenty. Whole armies have been crushed under your choice of weapons. Maybe it's just all the violence. You could make this simple, quick, and easy.

—*Go to* **PAGE 5**.

Or not. Just stay on this page of your life for a bit. Consider the ramifications. Close this story. Skip it. Do you need to see the end?

PAGE 4

This time you pull your head back slightly before snapping it forward again. Then, pushing him to the ground, you find your knees digging into his chest, your fists trading back and forth, left, right, left, right, left-right-left-right into his face over and over again. At some point, it becomes difficult to distinguish which sounds are coming from your own fists and which ones are coming from the pound of meat that is now his face.

Eventually, you look down at him and all you see is blood surrounding puffed up eyes, a slightly agape mouth, and the ears to frame it all. Ears that are pooling drop after drop of blood.

This is vengeance. This is what you were seeking. Everything you have done has led up to this point. The anguish in your life said press on, and you did. You pressed, and pressed, and pressed until the sack of shit you have before you was nothing more than a portion of the bloodlust you've had to get to this point. Each hit, each punch was for lives wasted. Lives you wasted in getting here, lives he wasted in his vainglorious grasp at power.

—*You've had enough of this. You need to walk away, go to* **PAGE 3**.
—*You've had enough of this. It ends now, go to* **PAGE 5**.

PAGE 5

With a sneer smeared across your lips, you stand up. Taking the knife from its sheath, you hold it up level with your gaze. It takes up the left side of your vision. He takes up the right. The blade is pristine. He's a crumpled mess. It's good. It's clean. He's finished.

As you slit his throat, you wonder what's next. What can you possibly do in your life to eclipse this? What did you solve? What did you gain?

War changes everything?

PAGE 6

He stares back, the fear in his eyes all too clear to see, the looks of grandeur and power he supposedly embodies reduced to nothing. However, as you continue to stare, all you see reflected in his eyes is power gone awry. Abused power that has led to ruined lives. Countless lives. All in the name of some ideal. Some invisible thread that strings together all the actions as if they are anything more than a cry of bloodlust covering corpses and maimed bodies.

You continue to stare into his eyes as a revulsion creeps into the back of your throat. At first it is a slight, unpleasant nudge. Then it grows until you feel it choking you. Gasping for air, you push him back while stumbling away from him. Putting your hands on your knees, you take a few deep breaths.

You're no longer facing him, but you can hear the sound of panicked shuffling and rasping sobs. He's crawling away. Eyes closed, you just listen for a few more seconds. This is the sound of a man brought low. A man who, if he continues to live, will seek to avenge himself on you one day. This is how the cycle continues.

You know you can't just walk away. After what he's done, there can be no forgiveness. After all *you've* done, there can be no going back. The only way forward is back toward him.

Pushing off your heel, you turn around and walk after him. His scurrying grows more frantic. While you stride forward with purpose, he stumbles, a suitable mockery of what once took place. He looks back, and meets your slitted eyes. Reaching him, you kick him down onto his stomach.

—*He must pay. Punch him. Go to* **PAGE 2**.

Unto Dust
Maddy Myers

Jackpot and I duck behind the pile of crates before the shots fire. I see him go down before I hear the guns. Safe.

"Raven," he chokes out. "I've been hit."

"How?" I whisper to myself.

"What the fuck?" he says. "I'm at 45% now. What the fuck happened?"

I stand up and throw a grenade. Then I duck back down again. My body starts shaking. I grasp a crate's edge and push myself back deeper into the pile. Pain begins to waver around the edges of my eyes. I look around in a panic.

"Jackpot?!" I wail. I can't see him. Has he already evaporated? Against my will and my better judgment, my body collapses to the ground. 5%. My arm, strong enough only to hold a pistol, shakes as I raise it. A figure rounds the pile of crates and stands over me. I hear his laughter through a hazy, thick buzzing in my ears. I aim the pistol at his head.

I fire. I watch the bullet go through his eyes.

And still, he laughs. Still, he stands. "Fucking noob," I hear him say, as I fade away. "Noob got pwned."

***

I spawn back at the base. Jackpot pats my back. "Hey, good work back there," he says. "I watched you on the camera feed before re-spawn."

"Thanks," I say. "I thought I got him."

"You didn't," he says. "No one can get him."

"What?"

"He's using some sort of ... I don't know, he's hacking. He's cheating." Jackpot straps on some armor. "It's not allowed on this server. He'll get booted."

"Are you sure?" I ask. "He's been top stats every time. I thought he was just good."

Jackpot stares at me. "We both watched you shoot him in the head," he says. "We both felt his bullets go through the crates. No one's that good. What, you've never seen a hacker before?"

"I have, once or twice, but what kind of hack makes it so that if someone shoots you, you live?"

"I don't know, invisible armor? I don't fucking know." Jackpot seems annoyed, all of a sudden. "What makes you think I know anything about how it works? I've never got one done. How should I know?"

"You said he was cheating, that's the only reason why I asked. Why are you mad?"

By the time I've finished the question, Jackpot has his back to me and he's twenty yards out. The round began a few seconds ago; the rest of the terrorists have made it halfway to the bomb by now.

I shuffle after Jackpot. I forgot to buy armor, but the shop has closed. I've got to run. I feel like taking out my knife and just waving its useless short range flash at enemies until the hacker gets the boot, but I don't. I'm too angry to fight and too angry for jokes. Usually, a hacker doesn't last this long. This all doesn't sit right with me.

I keep my sniper rifle out. I'll just play the turtle for now, hunched back in my shell and lining up shots from afar.

In the corner of my eye, I can see kill notifications blurring the top corner of my visor. The hacker is on the move. Headshot, headshot, headshot.

I stay where I am.

Headshot. This time, next to Jackpot's name.

I shift my weight. Jackpot is watching me on his retinal cameras before re-spawn, by now. He must be wondering why I'm still camping at the base. He must be grumbling that he taught me better than that.

I leap in the air, whirling until I feel dizzy, until I can't tell sand from crates from sky. I wait until the shot comes out of the air. Not a headshot, at least—I wouldn't give them that pleasure. I jump and jump again and make the process as trying as I can for the counter-terrorist cyborg.

The shot hits my leg first. I try to jump again, but my leg gives out, and a second shot hammers into my shoulder as I collapse. 2% health.

I can hardly see through the thick red haze. But, oh, that same voice in my ear again. That same laugh. He stands over me and takes out his knife. He crouches, again and again. He slices. He laughs.

***

"I can tell something's wrong," Jackpot says, "Because I can't feel a difference in the code."

The code. Always the code. He can feel it every time we boot up, he says. Scrolling through his brain.

"Can you feel anything?" he asks.

I shake my head. He was only posturing. He knows I can't feel the code, or at least, not enough to matter. I'm not an old enough model. Just DLC. A special addition. The latecomer. The noob.

Jackpot's memory contains bits and pieces of the earliest forms of the world. He was the first model made. He tells us stories of running through the streets of this city as it grew around him. He remembers and compares each update to the one before it, on and on until all the other teammates sigh, "Shut up, old man." I like his stories. He can always tell me how a map has been altered, even though the rest of us can only feel our memories clipping and blurring.

In the past, I've tried to watch the scrolling numbers behind my eyes during the world's occasional jumps and pauses. During updates, I can feel stops and starts twitching through my muscles, driving my blood in circles. But I can't tell the difference, in the end. I can never remember it, once the world comes back into focus and the round begins.

"Of course you can't," Jackpot spits. "You're still a nonbeliever, aren't you?"

"No," I say, avoiding his eyes, scrolling through armor upgrades. "I told you. I believe in the users now."

"Well, you don't believe in the developers," Jackpot shoots back. "You don't believe in our creators."

"It just seems ... disorganized," I say. "How could they let all of this happen? Users aren't just modifying maps anymore, they're modifying us."

"That's right, and we have no power to stop it," says Jackpot, his eyes narrowing to surly slits. "Not that we ever did. It's not our place. We have no power over anything we do here. You think you decide where to point your gun? They just pull our strings."

"See, that never made any sense to me," I say. "The users, the developers—which is it? Which one matters?"

"None of it matters anymore, apparently," Jackpot says, his voice low. He's throwing half his ammo on the ground, now. "In a just world, that hacker wouldn't be allowed to live. That asshole deserves a bolt of lightning from the sky. He doesn't belong here."

He runs ahead. I pick up the ammo he dropped. "I don't know about you," I call after him. "I control myself. I can control myself."

He grunts an inaudible reply.

"What?" I say.

The shots have begun. We've hung around the base too long. The counter-terrorists are already here.

I see Jackpot's body twitching, coiling into a fetal circle as he falls, too fast, to the ground.

For the first time since I ever spawned in the world, I close my eyes. I run back and forth in the darkness. I imagine the sound of bees in my ears, buzzing, blaring out the laughing cyborgs.

This isn't fun anymore.

***

Jackpot screams.

His arm is moving.

"I'm not doing it," he screams at me. "I'm not doing this!"

The arm draws his gun, points it.

I try to speak. My voice crackles like a rusted can. "What?!"

"I've been hacked! I've been hacked!"

He sounds on the edge of tears, his stony, square face stricken with shock.

"Do something," he says, shaking me with his good arm. "This thing...this isn't me. I didn't do this. I didn't put this in me!"

I stare.

He pulls away, paces.

"This must be a test of faith," he says, after a while.

I can hear the shots coming. Not far away now.

"We're camping," I say. "We can't stay here."

"I will overcome this," Jackpot says. "This is my choice. This is what I will do."

His arm raises and shoots through the wall. A headshot notification blares on my visor. His arm jerks left. Right. Headshot. Headshot.

He shoots through my body.

No friendly fire.

I fall to my knees.

"You're not hurt!" he cries. "I saw it! I saw it go...*through*."

I lie on the ground anyway. "Jackpot," I say. "I can't do this. I can't deal with this."

"What are you saying?" says Jackpot. Headshot. Headshot. His eyes focus on me, his arm moving without him needing to see where it goes.

The victory screen appears.

"What are you trying to say?" I hear his voice fade in and out as the kill counts display on the insides of my eyelids. Jackpot's arm killed them all. Every last one.

***

"Tell them to take me," I say, as the round restarts. I don't buy ammo. I take out my knife.

"Tell who?" says Jackpot. He looks afraid. I am afraid, too. My chest hurts from where the bullet went through it. An invisible, leftover pain.

"Tell the developers," I say. "Tell them to take my body. Make it into a different person. Tell them to take me out. Either that or give me the upgrade."

"I can't talk to them," says Jackpot, his voice cracking.

"You're a man of faith," I say. "You told me you knew them."

"Just the text," he says. "I've only studied the symbols. I don't know how to make them hear me."

"But they changed people here," I say. "The world changed us. I have to change, too. I can't keep up, anymore."

Jackpot can't hear me now. He's shooting through the wall again. I lie on the ground. I wait for him to finish beating everyone.

"Why is your hack so much better?" I shout over the shots. "Why are we winning?"

23

"I don't know," he shouts back. "Maybe I'm just that good?"

***

In the next round, Jackpot's legs are gone. The world has replaced them with sparkly sticks that hurt my eyes to look at directly. He clips the air as he jumps, too high to see. The world shatters around him into pieces. I blink and blink again as he jumps, my eyes unable to focus on him.

"Come back," I say, my voice feeble. But I don't mean it. I feel jealousy grow in the pit of my stomach.

He calls something from high above me.

"I can't hear you," I say.

The victory screen appears. I begin to understand.

He doesn't need me anymore.

***

I run ahead. I want to die. I want to watch the world through Jackpot's eyes, through the re-spawn camera feed. I have to be dead to see it.

I am tired of being alive, being safe, just sitting by as the world burns down and reconstructs again and again and again, so fast that it makes me sick.

I make it up to the crates and I wait. I hear shots, but far away, and behind me. Is Jackpot jumping and shooting? I won't be able to die and watch the world if he kills everyone too fast. The rounds go by so quickly now, I'll barely have a chance to see through his eyes before he ends it all and I'm jolted back to the spawn point again.

I run further ahead. Finally, I hear footsteps, but still no shots.

Why haven't they tried to kill me? Do they see me on their visor maps? They must know I'm not Jackpot. After all, they're still alive.

I pause. I take out my knife to show I'm not a threat, and I strafe around the corner.

A man has his back to me and his knife out.

I jump up and down, hoping he will hear me, but something feels wrong. He is too still, and he won't turn. And then, without warning, he runs. I watch a bullet zigzag through the wall and clip his shoulder.

I run past him, throwing my body in front of his knife. He backs away from me in a panic, slicing wildly. It's over fast.

***

I'm in the air, with Jackpot, soaring. The world looks like shimmery steel; buildings and walls waver, flickering in and out of being. The sand-swept inclined planes. The low rock walls. The pyramid of crates by the bomb site. The tiny counter-terrorists stumbling on their well-worn pathways, the old routes that made sense back when all of their enemies fought on foot. They are like mice in a maze now, or ants in a farm, trapped but still going through the motions. What else can they do?

I watch Jackpot's aim-assisted arm blast them out with slick precision. Headshot, headshot, headshot.

The victory screen feels too fast.

I want to stay up there with him forever.

***

"Jackpot, I don't think anyone is hacking anymore," I say.

"I don't think so either," he admits. I strap on armor. Jackpot goes bare-chested, now.

"You could stop using your powers," I say, a little too quiet.

Jackpot gives me a hard look. "What makes you think I can?"

"I don't know," I shrug. "I just mean, you don't have to jump all the time."

"We're winning, aren't we?" Jackpot says, his voice tight. "And anyway, I didn't ask for this. I can't control my arm anyway. I mean...it's not my arm. I didn't put this on. I was chosen."

I pause.

"Chosen," I say, at last.

Jackpot won't look at me.

"You really can't control it?"

Jackpot shakes his head.

"When you see the code," I say, "what does it look like?"

He meets my gaze. His eyes look tired. "It gives me a headache, now," he admits. "I can't look at it anymore."

"That can't be good," I say. "That can't be the developers."

"It could be," he says. But I can hear the doubt in his voice.

"It's the users," I affirm. "If this were the developers, if this was an update, then why can't the rest of us jump like that? This doesn't seem fair, you have to stop—"

"How many times do I have to tell you?" Jackpot has begun shooting. "I can't stop it. You can't stop it. We can't control anything here!"

I pause for a while, then I crouch and stand up again. I try to sense whether I am standing up, or whether someone else is standing up. I wave my knife in front of my face. Am I doing this? I feel a dull panic rising in my throat. Am I the only one in my head? How would I know if I weren't?

I try to think back to my first day, meeting the team, hearing Jackpot's gruff swears for the first time. He told me where to hide, when to strafe, how to jump. I didn't always do it right, and I still don't. I have good days and bad days. But everyone does, don't they? Or are my good and bad days the fault of someone else, some higher power that decides how well I fight?

My kill counts, my deaths, my stats—I see the numbers, I know they're real, I lived those experiences. I earn my victories, and when I have a rough day and feel too dizzy to aim straight, that's on me. Believing otherwise sounds like a cop-out, like making excuses. I own my mistakes.

Yet here was Jackpot, whose body had changed before my eyes, against his will. Or so he said. Did he really not choose this path? Could I get modified, too—cursed with powers by some unseen demigod?

I flash back to that sensation of floating in the air with Jackpot, seeing far-away dots moving on the ground. We didn't deserve that feeling. And yet no one had taken this power away from him. The world around us had broken, and no one had fixed it. How long could this go on?

I have to pray now for a miracle, even though that miracle would confirm my fear that I am not alone. This world has rules, rules that I had followed in spite of myself, all along. There are higher powers here. My victories are mine, but they are not *only* mine.

26

"I can hardly believe all of this," I say.
I wipe my eyes. Where is he?
"Jackpot?"

***

I walk out of the base.

I can't see a victory screen yet. Someone is still out there.

I walk slowly through the crate maze. I take my knife out.

In the hallway, I hear a soft rustle of movement. I move towards the noise.

Three men with knives have lined up at the end of the hall. They stare at me. I edge ever closer.

"Hello?" I call out.

I bounce in the air slightly.

"Hello," I say. "I'm sorry."

The one in the middle bounces back but remains silent.

"Let's just be normal," I say. Can they hear me?

The one on the left takes out his gun.

"Let's just be normal," I say again, more to myself. "There are no hacks on this server. Hackers get booted."

The pain comes slow and thick, in bursts. All three men have drawn and begun to fire. My eyes fill with blood. The world goes red, then black, then white, then the gold of stretching sand. I'm back at my camp again.

I close my eyes and let my body go still. I can almost feel the code. It feels safe. It feels balanced.

Ten Steps
Lana Polansky

He walks toward the same cave, in the same bushes, on the outskirts of the same town. Those are the same blue herons and tracks in the mud. The same grateful, young damsels eager to put themselves on display for him and only him. The same big blade slung over his back, the same pistol in his holster. He's only vaguely conscious of the sameness, of how every new step forward feels like trodden ground, of how the words in his head never quite feel like his own. He walks, or he is compelled to walk. He enters the cave, he removes the gun. He takes a remarkably familiar ten steps forward, but he doesn't remark it. He removes an elixir from a satchel he has never actually seen. He drops it on the ground.

He takes a step back, and the world crumbles away. The lines disappear, all the details shatter, and a fractal forms around him. Waves, diffraction, and eventually darkness.

The walls twist and the floor falls away. Colors mix and separate; lines blur, expanding and diluting from opaque saturation, dulling and greying, until they are imperceptible. The distinguishable world collapses into a color-faded soup.

He jumps, falling endlessly. He splays his arms like a heron, because there's nothing else to do. Waves radiate from his limbs, his head, the sharp angles of his body as he falls. Parts of him separate into the void. Dullness opens up to more dullness, spirals curl into deeper spirals. The world of rocks and trees and townsfolk and incongruities washes into a limbo. Everything falls apart. A world made infinite in a grain of sand, a world made of little grains, imploded.

The world goes black. . .

The world whirrs and buzzes and tries to start again.

He wakes up in the darkness. Something went wrong: a hiccup in the system, the fabric of his universe now thinned and frayed.

His eyelids brush against a cold, dark surface. *Cold*. He feels something all by himself. He lies there several moments, presses his hands, his body, his face onto the concrete. *Cold*. It shocks him into awareness of his own skin, his muscles, his veins, his heartbeat. He gives locomotion a try. A hero can move his own hands and feet.

He can hold up his own head. So the hero begins: he pushes himself up, falling onto his backside. He stabilizes himself with his hands almost involuntarily. Almost. He is aware of why he did it. His brain sent the message to his hands. He didn't know he had one, but the message was carried to it by his nervous system. It told him to stop from falling. He sits there a moment, eyes widened and fixating on nothingness. His hands planted on either side, his legs lying half-bent limply in front of him, he moves his neck. He feels the movement of his head, craning and flexing, looking up and down. A dim light trails across the floor that he wants to follow, highlighting the crevices and corners of the otherwise barren, cold, black cell. He's blessed with suffocating muscularity, but feels like bent straw. He pushes off with his hands, getting one leg bent up, the other resting on its knee. He rests his weight on the ball of his raised foot, holding himself, gritting his teeth, pulling both legs up uneasily, almost falling. With the same kind of involuntary yet deliberate action, his arms fan out on either side as he tries to find equilibrium, one foot in front of the other, shuffling forward. He feels as though he has never done this by himself before.

    He trips. He repeats the process. He falls, a tooth falls out and fades away. It hurts; it really hurts. He pushes himself up again and walks, following the dim light. He becomes more accustomed to himself, finding his gait, the barrel-chested gait of a hero, or something like that. The light leads to a slit in the darkness, becoming brighter and more distinctive as he approaches it.

    He catches his own shadow in the light. He has seen it before, but never took the opportunity to examine just how odd it looked. He doesn't really know why it's odd, just that it's so blocky. So jagged. It never swished and swayed elegantly like the others did. The strangers had nice-looking shadows. But his just sort of jarred frenetically, even when he was standing still. He never realized how self-conscious this made him feel.

    He has been watching it flicker on the ground for...who cares how long? The passage between one point and another was always so fluid, but the actual sensation of time—of slowness or speed—never crept up on him. Something would happen...and then it would stop. He would become fixed, like stone, until it started again. He could never control when it began or stopped, and it hardly mattered anyway. He always carried with him information from the last session, never knowing how it got there. He never knew how it stayed there, and he didn't know the difference between starting and stopping. Now he feels it so *viscerally*. There is a difference between the two, but he can't put his finger on it.

The hero walks through the crack tentatively. It's jagged like his shadow, but it's hot. Little, blocky grains of white light twitch and spill out. His body dissolves in the white grains, reforming on the other side as though all his molecules separated and reunited.

Familiarity washes over him. He feels the need to breathe. With his nostrils. His nostrils. He suddenly becomes aware of his nostrils. This world with rocks and trees and people makes him want to breathe in with his nostrils. He heaves, inhales the heady aromas of…

…Nothing. This familiar world smells like nothing. The void had more feeling. But. But. But maybe if he *touched* something? The grass? The green-gray grass sways elegantly in the scentless wind. He feels fairly confident about the grass. He kneels to touch it. His eyes widen, his lips curl into a pathetic, little grin. His hand wafts over nothing.

Nothing. All these new thoughts swishing into his brain make him self-conscious about the vapid ones he'd say aloud all the time, sometimes for no reason, sometimes while he was just running, or loading a gun. His rippling muscles—look at them! How they glisten! The bitches love them, just like they love a little tap on the bum. It was always assumed, and no one ever bothered to ask.

Nothing expands and warps in color. Suddenly the grass multiplies before him, prismatically spawning distinctively un-grasslike colors. The grass twitches and jars like a shadow, this little patch, multiplying into oblivion. The ground shakes under it, a ground he can't feel underfoot. He falls on both knees, looking out onto the spontaneous overgrowth.

"What are you doing, Bud?"

"…"

"I said, 'what are you doing?'"

Bud looks up at the old guru in the white gi. Wrinkling, wispily and balding, stoic and perpetually unimpressed. This was the place where he came to learn his formidable Kung Fu skills. He had never had a lesson with the man. He just ran the gauntlet tutorial until he could do it adequately enough.

But he hadn't used his mouth yet. He makes himself aware of all the tiny muscles in his face. He tries parting his lips, contracting those muscles around their contours, forcing the breath through his vocal chords to produce sound made audible in his throat and articulated by his tongue, until finally,

"Muuhhhhh...."

"We need you to clear out the cave." The master doesn't blink, doesn't flinch. He points to that same cave, down that same path, down the definitely different string of infinite grass now growing into the air. This is the part where Bud would run to it, gung-ho, kicking dirt up under his heels.

"Muuh...nammm...?"

"Come on. Let's go."

Getting himself up, Bud knows what would happen next. He would be led to the cave if he followed. So Bud sits down again. "What are you doing?"

And again. Standing up, then crouching again. Crouching here makes the master repeat himself. He *has* to repeat himself.

Standing up, then crouching again. Again, again, again, until it didn't matter anymore. The master can no longer control himself.

"I said 'what are you doing?' We need you to clear out the cave. Come on, let's go. What are you doing? I said 'what are you doing?' We need you to clear out the cave. Come on, let's go. What are you doing? I said 'what are you doing?' We need you to clear out the cave. Come on, let's go. What are you doing? I'm sorry. I said 'what are you doing?' We need you to clear out the cave. Come on, let's go. What are you doing? I said 'what are you doing?' We need you to clear out the cave. Come on, let's go. What are you doing? I said 'what are you doing?' We need you to clear out the cave. Come on, let's go. What are you doing? I said 'what are you doing?' We need you to clear out the cave. Come on, let's go. What are you doing?..."

***

Whenever Bud progressed to the cave before, he always sprinted. He didn't know why he always had to run everywhere, thinking about it now. But then, it doesn't look like there's much else to do but repeat himself or go forward to the marked place. As if the grand planner of Bud's destiny needed to lead him there by the hand. He takes his time, this time. He breathes in, slowly. No air, but little particles of the tiny, almost imperceptible squares collapse space around him like a crumpled piece of paper. They shoot through his mouth, through pores in the back of his neck, buzzing and stinging like shocks of electricity. Bud inches lumberingly toward the cave. He clutches his sidearm. Always there.

    Infinite overgrowth covers the mouth of the cave. He takes a step inside. He raises his gun. The place is eerily lit, crawling with mutants that abhor the light. Bud registers the guttural sounds and grotesque gestures in a way that makes him sweat and twists his stomach into knots. He feels the impulse to shoot when they approach, increasingly taking pity on them as bullets obliterate their disfigured bodies. How such a small bullet can annihilate a head so completely, reducing it to a firework of blood and rotten meat cubes. Every time he shoots, the bullet rips through the heaving, grasping mutants. Mutants with skin melting off their faces, so putrid in color that the ability to smell them would've been too much. They hopelessly lumber and swipe at Bud, eyes bloodshot or missing, mouths necrotic and decomposed, spilling with pus and bile. They moan, cry and spit and Bud can't help himself. He can't stand this feeling he gets for every single one he has to put out of its misery, looking at it in its useless face. It is programmed to see Bud as food. Sometimes it sneaks out of the cave at night. Sometimes it finds a fresh young virgin and makes a meal of her, dragging pieces of her back to the cave, like dinner was all she was ever made for.

    The others couldn't build a wall around the cave. Impossible. They couldn't send a mob to clear the cave themselves. Bud was the only one who could do it. The only one strong and brave and strapping enough. Something about this suddenly seemed cruel and absurd to him. Why is this where the town offloaded their sick? And why was their problem his problem? Because Bud can't move forward without first doing this. Bud pushes forward, compelled not to be grabbed, to find some answer before being pulled back into the dark abyss of a broken world.

    Each shot fired rips a hole through a creature, through some brownscale texture in the cave, firing infinitely, leaving behind it a trail of perforated universe. Every time he shoots, the bullet converges on a vanishing point in a darkened, back wall of the cave. Every bullet, hundreds and hundreds of them, disappear on some oscillating grid at the end of the semi-circular cavern. There is no other end to this place. Bud runs out of bullets, running, dropping the pistol to the ground where every slaughtered mutant part multiplies like the grass outside, creating infinitely growing trails and spirals of mucus and carnage which come to surround the cave until the brown-grey interior is saturated with blood reds and pea greens. Every time it crawls onto Bud it fades off, crawling back then fading again.

His pistol wasn't supposed to leave his side. It hits the ground fading, returning to his holster, magically, empty. No ammo refills anywhere. Bud pulls his Bowie knife from its sheath, running, hacking his way to the back wall.

He slashes the wall and the grid pulsates, gyrates and sparkles. He hits it again, again, again. More forcefully, more desperately, he keeps slicing the grid until it cracks and a great white light explodes through it, spitting out little, grainy particles. Like a vortex it begins to consume everything around Bud. All the same carnage and same stones and same flowers and the same master and the same damsels, sucked into the light, dissipating into particles, erased. Everything around Bud affects death as he holds on, resisting the force as much as he can, still awed by the beautiful white light.

Nothing exists around him but the light, the grid and the darkness. All the world around him falls away, and he is left with a void and one escape. The world isn't his anymore. It broke when he touched it. It felt empty when he perceived it. His whole body finally relaxes. His shoulders drop. He stops resisting. He had been coming here the whole time, anyway. He had to. He closes his eyes, smiling, and the warmth of the light embraces him, caressing his every particle until he fades into it completely.

***

"Uhhh, I think the disc is scratched," the kid whines. Annoyed, he whips his noise-canceling cans off of his head, hops over to his team coordinator, and hands her the disc.

"This build's pretty broken, you know?" she says, looking up at him incredulously.

"Yeah but I can't get this one to boot at all. It used to be alright but now it crashes as soon as I press start."

"Uh-huh."

The young woman with the frayed bun and smartly pleated pants takes a look at the disc. She's sitting in a similar swivel chair in a regrettably carpeted room. Rows of devkits are aligned in front of her against large plate-glass windows. She sits at a retractable table with her own kit. Her co-coordinator sits next to her, his angular, skinny face focused intently on a videogame. He's trying to make it past the cave level without incident.

"This game makes no fuckin' sense," he mutters.

"Do you know *how* it got scratched?" she inquires, eyebrow raised.

"No. Like I said, it was fine. I was testing a pretty bad out-of-world bug, then all of a sudden it stopped working and now there's a giant scratch on it." His hands are perched on the small of his back, his shoulders bobbing up and down in step to the anxiously hopping syllables.

Her eyes narrowing, she tries launching the disc on her console. Some buzzing and clicking, and then nothing happens. A minute or two of crashes and hard resets later, she presses "Eject" and pulls the disc from the tray.

"Yeah, this one's pretty dead. We'll see if we have another copy for you on hand."

"Thanks." The kid sighs.

The chronically exhausted coordinator knows the broken copy will have to be handled properly. As a third-party company, policy's strict. She sighs at the extra work of having to send a request for the useless disc to be obliterated, made unrecognizable, thrown in the garbage. She'll have to mark things down and color-code things and make it known that one disc was malfunctioning and missing and could a replacement be made because there aren't a ton of copies here? She sighs again. That out-of-world will need to be reproduced and reported and marked "A—Urgent" in the database. Not that the piece of shit will be ready for submission. Not that the devs seem to care all that much. Come Tuesday, the first Bud will be trucked off. The graves at the end of the death march will scatter the bottom of a landfill, resting eternally, in shiny little particles.

All Time Heroes
Matt Riche

He was dreaming again; the numberless grey foes screamed towards him, with the relentless patterned efficiency of marching ants. He was as fragile as they were, but unlike his enemy, he could see, and reason, and plan—they were slaves to their patterns, where he had the gift of reflexes and choice. One of him was worth a thousand of them.

Every night he blasted through them, his proud blue fighter-craft an extension of himself. The joystick, with its familiar click and rattle, was the point at which his body connected seamlessly to the things he saw. He knew their patterns, perceiving them not just with his eyes, but with his hands, and the map of bullet and flight patterns ingrained in his brain.

Though, in his dream, he inevitably reached the point where he finally succumbed. Some stray fragment or failed maneuver after a million perfect ones caused the tiny collision that led to his unceremonious, impotent whimper of a death.

JON awoke with a start. His brain echoed a noise from the haze of his sleep, a familiar yet unplaceable sound—like a little piece of metal tumbling down a tunnel. He blinked, reminding himself today didn't have to be the day the collision happened. He rubbed his hands into his face and took a breath, trying to purge the sticky film of sleep from his brain.

When idle, a pilot like himself would have no choice but to see the endless loop in his head. Everyone in his world would see this when they closed their eyes—the flashing colors meant to attract and entice a soul to become a player, to contend in the battle to Save Our World, or to set the highest score doing so.

JON stretched and instinctively hit a button on the wall of his quarters. The big screen quietly zapped a static fuzz over itself, and the numbers and letters faded slowly onto the screen, almost as slowly and sleepily as he had awoken.

TODAY'S HEROES
1. JON - 99929520
2. A.M - 99510060
3. RET - 90004480

That there, that was his identity. To become number one, you had to want only that, and live only that.

Mr. Number One left his room and padded barefoot out to the kitchen of the opulent quarters the fleet provided him, near Area 16, the so-called "Final Area." Today, he was going out to do Area 16 again for what would be the third time. He switched on all the CRT monitors in every room as he walked by, their barely audible static squeal making him feel less alone. JON was indeed number one among "Today's Heroes." But who was number one today wasn't yet immortal, like those who lived among the All Time Heroes.

JON waited a moment for the screen to scroll to the next scoreboard. The one that changed far less. The one that honored the dead.

ALL TIME HEROES
1.   J.S - 999999040

***

Long ago, J.S was the first player to see Area 16. When he approached the end of the area, the audience waited with bated breath. His skills were spectacular. J.S had brushed aside wave after wave, deftly making a path through the haze of projectiles as they created curves and sine-waves in the sky.

Amid J.S's seemingly never-ending struggle, the warning klaxon finally came. The Mothership approached, big and angry-red, spewing bullets in kaleidoscopic swathes. It looked like the other motherships, but recolored with a more sinister palette. At that time, no one had seen a red one before. J.S was cool-headed and untouchable. He seemed to dance between the points of light forever until the satisfying sound of explosions, almost playfully rewarding, rang out against the chaos. The red Mothership faded away. The people rejoiced.

As the story goes, J.S remained still, knowing something didn't feel right. He waited, cruising through the blackness.

The enemy sent a message.

"WE ARE NOT DEFEAT. YOUR WORLD HAS NOT SAFE! TRY AGAIN!"

J.S had feared this. Area 16 was the "last" area, but beating it didn't make the fight stop. The waves came again, just like in Area 1, in an infinite loop. The people's hearts all died a little when J.S took out the Mothership. Once it was known that another Area 1 lay beyond Area 16, they all knew it could never stop. J.S fought through Area 16 again, watching the Mothership break apart once more. And then he faced another force of foes at another Area 1.

J.S slipped, finally, on his third trip to Area 16. It wasn't a mothership, it wasn't even one of the nastier waves. It barely made a sound when he died. Their hail of bullets ended the great hero, but the drones just kept flying, buzzing around relentlessly, mechanistically.

***

JON made his coffee, his hand twitching as if it were hovering over the joystick. He saw the foes, buzzing around like hornets, whenever he closed his eyes. It was time to challenge J.S's legacy.

A tone came from a speaker on the wall. JON hit the intercom button.

"Hey! It's DAV."

"Hey."

"You're doing Area 16 today, right?"

"...Yeah."

"The big day," DAV said excitedly.

"Do you want something, DAV?"

"Yeah. I want to do Area 16 with you."

"No, DAV."

"Come on, man. I'm not letting you go alone this time. J.S went alone and we both know what happened to him."

"Maybe I'm better than J.S," JON said, flatly.

"We both know it's not worth it. I'm coming and we're doing a run together. We'll see what's beyond 16-3."

"1-4. That's what we'll see. We'll just go back to 1-4," JON muttered exasperatedly.

Then, like every clockwork morning, he drank more coffee, did some stretches, and grabbed some fresh clothes. JON was ready to head out into the station and make the preparations for his run.

Before he went to the door he be paused, and waited, for the scoreboard to roll past in his mind's eye.

AREA 16
1. JON - 99929520

Still number one. Soon he'd clear one-hundred-million.

He opened the door and headed out into the station.

"JON! JON!" came the cheers of excited voices. Men and women alike cheered for JON, in a fandom he sometimes thought was senseless.

"I love you, JON!"

JON just waved and smiled. He loved the shouting and the praise. They'd ask how he got so good at flying, how many he could take out, how delicately he could thread his path through bullet hell. Sometimes, he'd look twice, trying to understand what he saw in their eyes—Adoration, pride, wonder? Jealousy, fear, worry?

Other pilots saluted JON and clapped. They could see the stats, the flashing marker above his head. People shouted encouragement and praise as he walked through the promenade.

"JON!"

DAV rounded the corner.

"I'm warmed up and ready! How about you?"

"I had my coffee. My trigger finger is loose. Are you sure you have to do this?"

DAV's face was a mix of pride and annoyance with his friend.

"I know you can probably survive this on your own, but I won't let the world's favorite pilot risk his life while I sit here."

"It's *you* risking *your* life that's the problem," said JON.

"I'm not the world's favorite pilot."

A smile crept through JON's persistent frown.

JON and his wingman approached the hangar together. There was an old man looking at JON with a glare of disapproval. JON looked back, waiting for the look in the old man's eyes to change when he realized *just who he was staring at*. But the old man kept staring him down, as if he had done something wrong.

"Stats..." JON thought. He looked up at the old man, this time with his stats overlayed on JON's vision.

AREA 2

59931. AAA - 000001580

"Bloody quitter!" DAV spat on the floor by the old man's feet.

"How can a quitter dare show his face, huh? How can he look at you like that, with what you're about to do? Made Area 2 and gave up. What kind of life is that? Who'd even be able to wake up and face the day with that many zeros floating above their head?"

JON didn't have an answer.

The two pilots passed through the hangar door and walked down the lit walkway to their crafts. JON stepped up to his slick, beautiful, blue fighter. Its wings sang of majesty to JON. He adored that jet for all the victories it saw him through, for how it made him feel so free and strong.

JON sat as comfortably as he reasonably could in the cockpit and hit the start button. The fighter was pulled automatically along the runway by the mass-driver. The fighter was pushed across the hangar toward the launch bay doors. Coming up right beside him seconds later was DAV's candy-red fighter, a perfect copy of his blue one.

A detached, yet soothing feminine voice emanated from the computer:

"One, Ready."

JON hit the ignition.

"Two, Ready."

DAV did the same.

The soaring white noise deafened them as they launched.

Through the glass before his eyes he could see the stars passing by, along with the HUD reading "AREA 16."

"You know the drill," JON reminded his wingman. "Don't look *at* the bullets, look *through* them. See it all at once."

"I know, I know. This ain't my first rodeo either, punk."

And then the hornets came, streams of them faster than he had ever seen before.

His dream flashed behind his eyes. JON tensed, slapping his own face to correct himself.

JON and DAV tore through the waves, matching them with equal zeal. They flew so fast. They could take so many hits before they'd break. JON and DAV pulled their fighters back to put as much space—and bullets—between them and the rapid enemy cascades as possible.

"Watch your six! Don't go too far back!"

In Area 16, they liked to sneak up. JON never once let his concentration lapse. He remembered where they liked to pop out.

JON often wondered what really happened to J.S that day. Was it really too difficult? Or was something on his mind? Was he distracted? Did he just lose his patience?

The enemy fighters clustered up into a tighter formation, all occupying the same space, making a big crunchy mass for JON and DAV's bullets to tear at.

What was he at? It had to have been over one-hundred-million now. Was it all nines? Or would he be the first man to have that tenth digit? He wanted to see the stats, but the distraction might kill him. JON never broke his own rules; he never took his eyes off the combat.

Did J.S worry about the same thing?

He pushed the thought aside. Still more drones coming. There were always more coming.

Room to move was getting scarce. The enemy's patterns pushed almost to the nose of his fighter, threatening collision, only exploding at the last second as he frantically tried to dig out some space between himself and their endless armada.

It looked like it wasn't even fair, like it wasn't even possible. They were faster and tougher than Area 16 at the end of the second loop. Area 16 at the end of the third loop had to be the last one, because a fourth Area 16 would likely be unbeatable.

"No..." JON whispered.

His calm broke and he was losing control—for the first time in ages, he began to panic. They were too tightly packed, and they were coming too close before he could destroy them. A collision was imminent. There were two ways out of a run—a pilot either made it through the area and returned to the station, or the pilot spent his last moments in his fighter. It was getting to be too much, even for JON. Today was the day it happened.

Then it stopped, and there was a silence.

Then came the klaxon.

"Mothership!" DAV choked.

"Oh god."

JON looked at the stats.

1. JON - 99999700

He had edged past J.S's score, but he couldn't revel in it just yet. The angry, red thing was coming.

The sounds of the lasers and volleys of shots were muted to him. JON let his mind go free, sensing what to do, eyes glazing over, and engaging the synapses of his brain specifically for this moment. He let bullets graze the sides of his fighter gently as if there were no danger in it. He hammered the glowing weak spot of the Mothership with infinite rounds of bullets every chance he got, daring more and more each time, so greedy to destroy that it was beginning to overcome his instincts to protect himself.

And then, the satisfying sound of the explosion, crunching white noise slowly fading into tiny pops and blips, until the one-hundred-million pieces of the ship disappeared.

JON's heart leapt. He had outdone J.S, outdone his own subconscious. Would he retire? Or would he...

JON - 00000250

He was confused. Frozen.
"DAV, my score...what do you see?"
"You're at...00000250..."
"DAV, what happened?"
"You got more than 99999999...I guess that's...what happens."

JON walked through life with his worth proudly displayed above his head. *But that's when the first digit was a nine.* Now, he might as well be at the beginning of his career, for all it mattered.

He had wanted his score next to the man he admired. He wanted his score next to J.S's. Now it wouldn't even be on the board.

"What will I do now?" asked JON. His friend had no answer.

Then came the transmission.
"WE ARE STILL NOT DEFEAT."
They hung there in the blackness.
"Does it matter what I did?"

41

"I saw it, man," said DAV, "I'll make sure everyone knows you're the first one."

"But the hall of fame. I can't get in. No one will remember this."

"Is that a bad thing, JON?" asked his friend.

"I don't know. What will people say?"

He could have at least rested in the Top 10 if they had just managed to take his life sooner. The enemy let him down.

"JON, my hands are cramped. I've got to take a break. I'm headed back."

JON sat, thinking for a moment about showing his face at the station with a number like 00000250 above his head. It now occurred to him how many people he had judged for having too many zeroes leading their score.

"Are you coming?"

In this silence, in all his confusion, JON's hands didn't stop their twitching, their hunger to dodge and weave and return fire. He urged to watch the score climb. He could hear the sound of the white noise as the drones died by his hand.

Watching the score climb, for all these hours...

"I've been so stupid..." JON said. DAV didn't respond.

"This is all for me." he whispered. His Player 2 remained silent.

"All those zeroes. All those zeroes, right next to my name."

"The system can't even handle what you can do...no one was prepared for you to come along!" DAV's voice seemed unsure if this was glory or the moment JON's life was crumbling.

JON didn't move a muscle—he was frozen, gripping the stick as if it was still all happening, as if his body didn't know anything else.

Who else had rolled back to zero? Anyone who did would not make it into the Hall of Heroes—the number of times they had beaten Area 16 would never have been recorded. Maybe JON wasn't the first. Maybe JON wasn't the one-hundredth. Maybe J.S wasn't the greatest. Maybe the greatest was some unnamed soul whose name never graced the All Time Heroes.

"JON?" DAV called out meekly.

"Maybe..."

JON thought an empty, profound, cold thought, and hesitated a moment before speaking that thought out loud.

"...Maybe this is pointless."

The Hierarchy of Needs
Ian Miles Cheong

John Hurst awoke at 8:00 a.m. His Bathroom meter was in the yellow, so he went to the bathroom. His Hygiene meter was in the red, so he took a shower. His Hunger meter was also in the red, so he made himself a sandwich, almost starting a stove-top flare-up. They shot back up to green when he was done. It should have been an ordinary day, but then with nary a sound and little excitement, the toilet disappeared.

He lived alone after graduating from university. Having spent all the money he had, Hurst had just moved into his suburban bungalow in sunny Sunset Valley. He was eager to meet his neighbors, the Landises, the Tennos and the Garths, who were equally eager to give him a housewarming as soon as he arrived. He was happy to get to know them, and did his best to ingratiate himself to them with conversations, hugs, and a BBQ party.

It took only two weeks for John to get promoted. It was an unbelievable stroke of luck, but he never questioned his good fortune. Things happened quickly where he lived.

It seemed like life was a simple series of events. Even his job consisted mainly of binary choices. All he had to do to earn his promotion was to do a bit of reading and some exercise, and to befriend his neighbor, Morton Garth, who also happened to be his boss. Becoming friends with Garth involved little more than talking about the weather, it seemed. The weather was always pleasant, and they had pleasant conversations, so Hurst had no complaints.

When he wasn't at work, he was at home, either watching his Fony TV or reading books on his Relax-o-Matic sofa to increase his Skill metrics in practices his boss deemed necessary for further job promotions. This time, he was working on Creativity and Fitness.

He spoke to the Garths to ask if they noticed their toilet disappearing also, but none of them seemed to have any idea what he was talking about. They seemed content to discuss the weather. It was the same with his all his neighbors, none of whom seemed inclined to even humor him. If they knew anything, they weren't saying so.

He didn't give it much more thought and went off to work.

When he returned home, things took a turn for the bizarre as soon as he stepped through the front door. His bathroom meter was approaching yellow again from the long day; he felt compelled to search for a toilet, but dimly remembered he didn't have one any longer.

John stomped his foot like a toddler and groaned something in a language that sounded a little like French at his unfulfilled need, but what frustrated him more was his inability to communicate his utter confusion. But who would he have to talk to anyway?

When he turned around again, his living room had become a long, windowless corridor lit only by lamps on the wall. He walked down this long corridor only to find a junction of two paths going left and right. He needed badly to pee, but his Hunger meter took priority, and he knew instinctively that he had to turn right if he wanted a bite to eat.

As he turned right, he walked down another long corridor and found a door at the end leading to a makeshift kitchen containing nothing but a fridge and a kitchen counter. As he made himself a sandwich, he began to wonder why things were where they needed to be, and how he knew exactly where to go. He began to realize that he had never made a decision on his own, and had this been an ordinary day, he wouldn't have minded.

"What the fuck is going on here?" He complained loudly to himself.

After consuming his meal, he still needed to deal with the tyranny of his throbbing Bathroom meter, which nearly drowned out his sense of injustice at how he was unable to relieve himself wherever, or whenever he wanted.

"Would it be so wrong to take a piss in the corridor?" He wondered aloud.

He walked back down the long corridor to the junction and headed down the other path, where he suspected there would be a makeshift bathroom.

As he walked further down the new corridor, he heard a thundering jolt behind him. Turning around, he saw that the walls he had passed were no longer there. In their stead was a huge gaping hole where walls were moving and repositioning into a maze. His brain wanted him to flee, but his legs couldn't.

Hurst had no choice but to keep walking down this new corridor, which was as doorless and windowless as the one before, only it seemed to maze left and right at every other juncture with no discernible pattern. It appeared, though, that the scenery was blending together in an endless loop.

Egged on by his bladder, he walked for a few hours, hoping for a change of pace with every occasional turn left or right, still unable to relieve himself. Even so, he knew that he could lose control of his bladder right then and there but chose not to, out of simple shame. Taboo was not a new concept to him. It had been assimilated into his functions for as long as he could remember. It was as if he had been programmed to feel it, and he gave into that impulse.

"What's happening?" He wondered aloud. His biological functions were the only things keeping him from getting "lost" in this hellish maze. Yet, at the same time, he had come to realize that were it not for his biological functions, he would have been able to attempt escape of the maze by walking in a direction not plotted out by whoever was designing it.

He felt helpless. The meter was almost empty, deep in the red. He couldn't hold it anymore. It needed to be green again or he would burst. He couldn't help it. He lost control, right then and there. It wasn't something he did willingly, and he felt the pain of shame as he wet himself all over the corridor.

"Ah, fuck you!" He cried in anguish to no one who would ever hear it.

At that point, a door appeared in front of him which lead to the outside world. He was free, but he didn't know what to do with himself. The maze transformed back into his comfortable, familiar home. His humiliation would fade into another memory, like graduation day and the big move to sunny Sunset Valley.

The very next day, he couldn't shake the knowledge he had gleaned, but he knew that there was nothing he could do about it. Instead, he asked the Garths about the weather. It was pleasant.

Slow Leak
Rollin Bishop

But when he knew he heard

Odysseus's voice nearby, he did his best

to wag his tail, nose down, with flattened ears,

having no strength to move nearer his master.

—Homer, *The Odyssey* (1049–1052)

    Of everything, the sky is what I find hurts the most. The people, the places, the various thoroughfares…Those are the kinds of things that come and go on a fairly regular basis. Folks leave; buildings are torn down; streets are renamed or diverted. The sky, though. Well. The sky is a thing of beauty that shifts in color but never really leaves. That's what I might have said before. Then it left.

    Not all at once. If it'd gone that quickly, we'd have noticed. The stars were snuffed out one by one, then by the handful, and finally even the moon was gone. It was only as the last few twinkling lights were burning out that the bits and pieces came together to form a cohesive whole.

    The days were full of questions. Folks congregated en masse at city hall only to have their concerns rephrased and repeated back to them. The best they could do was tell us that we should just stay inside and wait it—whatever it was—out. The mayor said she'd already been in contact with mayors from neighboring towns and would let us know as soon as she'd heard back from them. She finished her speech by telling us we worried too much.

    Then people started to disappear.

***

    Our town never had been a populous place. It was really just an extension of the two towns to our north and west. As folks moved south from the one, and east from the other, the two dozen or so of us decided it was about time we had a mayor of our own.

We all just referred to our little patch of real estate as Southeast, as something of a glib reminder of our origins.

That two dozen soon became three dozen. Small businesses began to sprout on every corner. A drugstore here, a comic shop there. And the kids. The kids were probably the best thing about it. There's always something joyous about watching children make discoveries of their own. Though I never did have any of my own (not for lack of trying, mind) the gaggle of pint-sized monsters kept me busy when I volunteered to watch them. It was enough, for a while.

Then times got hard. Folks left, stopped calling on each other. Our happy little town became a place of doldrums, filled with nothing but memories of better times. When I asked the mayor what'd happened to cause such a rift, she shrugged at me and said, "Hard to get people to stay when there's always somewhere to go." I reckon she was right.

So it came to be that there were only a grand total of eight, counting the mayor, when the stars went dark. The stores had been all boarded up for a long time, and we mostly kept to ourselves. I would ask the mayor what she'd received back from the other towns, but she always said that there'd been no word. After a week, I got worried. After three, so did she. We'd both failed to notice at the time that three of our meager group had joined the stars, wherever they were.

Eight had become five. Then the power went out.

***

After the power went, and didn't come back, I hesitantly asked the mayor what we'd do when all the food was gone. She gave me an incredulous look, raised a brow and told me, "What makes you think you need it?" I stopped eating after that.

The nights weren't dark so much as they were absent. Without the stars, moon, or power, it was like the world ended each time the sun went down. Each morning, those of us left would congregate at the hall. There were only three of us when the buildings started to go. First it was all those rundown shops that hadn't seen use in ages. Then, one by one, the abandoned houses were gone.

I quietly came to terms with the fact that I'd probably be one of the next to go. Fear seemed like a curious thing more than a fact of life. Why be afraid of something when you're certain it's going to happen? When I stopped eating it didn't stop the hunger. I apparently didn't need the food, but I certainly wanted it. The cold nothingness would be a welcome reprieve from the endless gnawing sensation in the pit of my stomach.

Somewhere during that feverish time the last of the townsfolk slipped out of existence.

Then it was just the mayor and me, left to wait.

***

When the sun finally didn't bother to even come up, the mayor and I bunkered down in the candlelit portions of city hall, both for the sake of our sanity and because my house finally drifted off to join the others. The darkness encroached upon the doors but went no further. The candles and lanterns the mayor lit stayed that way. I would have asked how but, to be honest, I was a little afraid of the answer. Instead, I quietly suffered my hunger and let her do as she pleased.

Her office quickly became a pile of pages, full of calculations and strange words. She'd taken to mumbling about "servers" and "admins" while doodling equations and maps at all hours. The constant hunger finally subsided into one long, hollow feeling, and her behavior became more overtly erratic. When I did eventually try to intervene, she shrugged me off. Then, as if something had suddenly struck her, she straightened and stared me down, taking my measure.

"I'm going to make you a mod," she said. I told her that was fine and dandy, but it didn't mean a thing to me. She chuckled before returning to her work. I curled up in the corner, ultimately too tired to fight her turn to whimsy, and fell asleep. When I awoke, I wasn't hungry anymore, but the mayor was gone.

She'd left a note on her desk. "Off to find other admins," it read. "No hope of bringing the servers back up without them. Hold the office till I return. I'm sorry to put this on you but there was no other choice. I'll be back as soon as I can. Promise." I folded the note up and stuffed it in my pocket.

She'd be back. She promised. I just had to wait.

***

So here I am. Present, I guess. Time's fuzzy without the sun or moon cycling through the void that used to be the sky. Don't rightly know how long it's been since she left. Just know I want her to come back. Don't feel hungry, or tired, just... sad. I cry when I feel up to it, quietly, and then stop when I can't any longer. Sit in the chair watching the door. Nothing happens. It's been too long. She isn't coming. Perhaps someone, anyone at all, will find this among the mayor's unintelligible doodles.

Just want it to be over. Want it to end. Nobody here anymore. Not even me. Just an empty room. Empty room and a door. Just close my eyes, maybe. Maybe see what everyone else is seeing. What's the point? Point stopped existing a long time ago. Time to stop. Time to end this. Sounds good. Sounds so good.

I imagine her opening the door. Put a smile on my face one last time. Bliss. "I waited for you," I'd say. "I waited."

If the Sun Rises Again
Dylan Sabin

When had he last seen a pilgrim ascend the snowy path? Had it been days? Weeks? Would he ever see the sun again? He found he had been asking himself these questions more and more as time wore on.

His wits and strength were tested when he overthrew the age-old evil infesting the mountain's peak. He felt the heat of a rising sun on his heavy armor, heard the crunch of snow under his near-comically oversized boots. As swords were swung and his enemies fell before him, the threat that once plagued the world was extinguished.

For centuries, every last villager was terrified of the mountain. They lived in hushed solitude, huddled within the confines of the walled villages bordering that fearsome slab of rock and snow. He'd arrived from a land far away to rescue them, armed at the outset with nothing more than a rusty sword and a worn pair of leg plates. Without assistance, he climbed that ominous crag and became the savior for an entire race of helpless pilgrims.

As he made the climb, the sun blazed above, inching higher and higher with each step he took. After a time, he noticed that the sun moved at a speed relative to his rate of progress. The longer and more often he moved forward, the closer the sun approached its apex.

At the top of the mountain was perched a throne of stone, a seat from which the mountain's ruler could see a panorama of the land below. He earned his title by savagely tossing the mountain's previous owner off the edge. The sun was at its highest when he claimed the peak, a shining beacon that cast down its approval upon him as he stared at the stone slab.

Rumors abounded that this seat allowed one's senses to be heightened far beyond natural ability, this power coming only at the cost of being locked to the chair for an indefinite length of time. This was a rumor he was willing to both believe and accept as he took the few needed steps to place his plate-guarded rump upon the slab. He shouted as best he could, a booming baritone voice rolling down the mountain to signify that he had saved the world.

As news spread across the land, pilgrims started making their way up the mountain, excited to see what wondrous things were along the most treaded path. They joyously broke down their obsolete village walls. With no snarling evils to harm them, these well-off yet doe-eyed citizens could make it to the peak without fear, eager to heap praise and gifts upon their savior. He accepted both willingly, and why wouldn't he? After all, he rescued these villagers from the constant threat of monsters rampaging down from the mountain. He saw dignitaries, artisans and commoners alike; anyone able to make the climb shared something with him. Anything he needed or wanted was brought to him: food, literature, exotic new weaponry, all manner of mortal delights were on display for him from his peak atop the mountain.

The role of a diplomat was a much simpler life than he expected so soon after setting out from his home. He still hoped for struggle and conquests to last him a lifetime, not an early shift to silver platters and wheels of cheese. There was so much more to the world that he could see, but couldn't touch and experience for himself. He could hope for little more than sitting on this throne as unending day stretched on.

In many ways, he'd become a part of the community without wanting to. He offered advice on political conflicts he had no business getting involved with and counseled citizens who could likely get through their days without his intervention. Whenever he started reconsidering his involvement, a new crisis arose to force his hand. The tittering voice of doubt was drowned out by the needs of his subjects.

Time passed and the sun refused to set, blazing high above the peak of the mountain. It led the commoners to strengthen their belief in his power: surely it was he who brought them the gift of light. They praised him and the sun alike, showering more needless tribute upon him while he remained comfortable and calm upon his throne. Trickling thoughts of complacency began burrowing into his mind, a siren's call leading him to wonder if he would live out the rest of his days with such simplicity.

Eventually, the sun began its dawdling decline and he started to worry. Visitors to the peak were slowing in frequency and he could see the specter of doubt in their gaze, sensed the caution in their prostration and tribute. When he peered down into the valley, his picturesque view was tainted by scraps of wood and steel coming together over time, forming the base of new walls along the edges of villages both near and far. He questioned the citizens who came to praise him, but they gave no answers to their once-fearless savior.

It was unfathomable, surely. He'd *rescued* them from the jaws of tyranny. Were they growing afraid of *him*? Did they expect him to turn on them just like the tired, old creature that he had deposed? How preposterous! They were his flock, subjects and citizens alike. He'd saved them, brought them the gift of light...but now that gift was leaving them.

He sat atop his throne of stone, preparing himself for a day when no one would come to visit him. He felt his tone growing shorter as he spoke with the petty rabble. If they were going to stop believing in his superiority, why would he waste any more time with them than necessary? They gave their gifts, asked their pointless questions and moved down the mountain, back towards their hovels and their walls. Let them leave.

The sun moved further down, inching ever closer to the horizon. As it made its slow decline, the number of villagers approaching him ground to a halt, much as he'd feared. Only one pilgrim came to visit him lately, a haggard old woman he'd never seen before, dressed in thick heaps of cloth. She took a seat in front of him, straining to keep her legs crossed and eyes drawn downward, refusing to address him in the frightened manner most commoners used in the interminable stretch of time that was the sunset. Minutes, perhaps hours passed while they sat in each other's company. The warrior wondered how much time he had before the sun vanished entirely. He questioned her motive; her demeanor and the noticeable lack of burden on her shoulders were entirely foreign. Even the poorest civilian brought *something* to him, but she traveled with only the robes on her back.

When the woman decided to speak, the tone she used caught him by surprise. It was level, almost calculated in its austerity, but the intensity in her eyes worried him the most.

"You near the end of your journey. The mountain has been kind to you, has it not? It showers you with gold, towers of equipment and weapons like no man could hope to see again. When commoners saw nothing but fear and despair, you brought them the sun.

"You have accomplished the impossible, Danethor the Strong. I say this not to exaggerate or overstate your efforts; if anything, my words couldn't be more precise. Have you paused once since you rested upon that throne to question the sheer absurdity of what you have done?" He looked at her with contempt, unable to piece together what she was saying. Her words sounded like the maddened gibbering of someone with sunstroke.

"A thousand creatures roamed this mountain, their aims guided by a single monster who sat where you rest now. You tore them apart one by one, surviving every encounter without a scratch. At no point did you pause; at no point were you forced to relent and move back down the ascent. Nobody in this land would dare step foot within a mile of the mountain's base, and you did so with ease, with callous disregard for your life. Why?"

It was a question he never considered before or after his ascension. There was but one goal when he arrived here, his whole essence devoted to freeing this mountain from its tyrannical, monster-spawning monarch. That relentless pursuit was his one constant, but as to why he'd come here in the first place, no answers sprouted from his mind. This angered him more than he expected, his brow furrowing as he gave a dismissive gesture. "Be gone from my sight, hag. Insolence is not a proper tribute."

"Think back," she began, standing up and looking past the throne, "can you remember anything before setting foot on the mountain's base? Can you piece together a single instance—"

"*Leave!*" He couldn't help yelling now, that booming baritone voice cascading down into the valley and frightening the commoners below as it cracked with worry. "Your words are meaningless! This is my domain now: I have rescued this land from its oppressors. You will not change that!"

"I will leave, but first I must ask you this: what will happen if someone sees *you* as the oppressor, Danethor the Strong?" She started down the hill, passing out of his sight without so much as a farewell. As she moved past a large spire, he felt a chill running down his spine. A brief glance backwards confirmed his worst fear: the sun was set at last, every last inch of radiance obscured beyond the horizon as the land fell into twilight.

Now he sat there, supernaturally adhered to a slab of granite and abhorring his decisions more by the minute. When he first saw the throne, sitting on it seemed natural the moment the previous occupant met her end on the rocks below. Now, the twin voices of doubt and self-deprecation gnawed through the recesses of his mind. He made a soft grumble, finding that his voice still carried further than he cared for. The echo rolled down the mountain slopes, turning into the briefest hints of thunder as they approached the nearest villages.

He hadn't seen a soul near the peak in the time after that strange woman appeared, and since then he'd sat in this endless night with only the wind and his thoughts to keep him company. Keeping track of time seemed pointless now, as did worrying about the plight of the villagers who abandoned him. They'd survived well enough without his aid before, surely they could continue on after abandoning his wisdom.

With all the time in the world left to spend with himself, the nagging voices in his head now asked him questions he could no longer ignore. If time moved forward with any reason, he surmised that a few weeks had passed since the old woman delivered her cryptic monologue. The ticking of his internal clock was no longer what concerned him, too nebulous was the quiet of this endless night.

He could not remember the briefest second of a time before he started up this mountain. Each step of that journey was clear in his mind and filled him with vigor, but trying to dig further back resulted in nothing but a fierce headache. He strained and scratched at his brain to remember his homeland, his parents, his schooling—anything that wasn't directly tied to this mountain. It took all he had not to scream.

He lifted his hands to his helmet, a proud shell emblazoned with gold etching and silver signets. With little effort, he lifted it off and tossed the steel to the snowy ground. It clanged weakly as it rolled away, kicking up and crunching snow before settling to a stop. The wind picked up and he could feel the frigid breeze on his scalp. Near-arctic chills rushed through a head of matted brown hair.

Forsaking just one piece of equipment felt strangely cathartic. The bitter irony in its new location just a foot or two out of his reach made him regret sitting down once again. His hands went to a shoulder plate, this one given to him by one of the wealthiest nobles below. It joined the helmet.

A thick steel gauntlet crashed on the ground as he felt the voice of doubt bubbling up to whisper to him once again; this time, he was in no mood to shut it out. It spoke to him in slithering tones, words passing through some sort of tainted sludge before reaching his ears. The question it asked was one he'd considered only once, refusing to think about its implications.

Had his purpose been solely to rise to the peak of this damnable mountain? It was a task only he could have accomplished, he admitted with reservation, but his life was meant for more than that, wasn't it? He removed his other glove and tossed it further than the first, lamenting all the adventures he couldn't have, would not experience because *this* was the story he had made of his life.

"Danethor the Strong, fearless savior and champion of the mountain," he uttered with a sigh, "stuck to a bench for all eternity."

The second shoulder plate hit the ground with a resounding clank, clattering against the steel of a gauntlet. That noise was followed by the unlocking of his chest plate, a towering heap of steel littered with sharp edges and sharper inscriptions. His armor seemed superfluous now, an obsolete relic. The bright steel glittered in the light of the moon, but he knew its time in the spotlight was up. He lifted the chest plate over his head and threw it to his side, not caring in the slightest that it careened off the edge of the peak in a violent plummet to the rocks below.

Both fur-lined boots slid out from embracing his feet with ease; he sighed with relief as he wiggled his toes in the frigid wind. He felt colder without the embrace of his armor, but the physical stress he endured from the mountain winds were only an echo of the storm in his mind. He grumbled again, loud enough to hear the thunderous callback as it carried down to the villages and hovels below.

He heard of the local religion in his talks with nobles and preachers, back in the time when he wasn't left to his own devices. There was one god in their world, a nameless figure who guided their hands when they needed it most. This figure was more than a mere representation, preachers told him in confidence, of an individual's ability to find strength within themselves. Danethor thought their notions a bit ridiculous, as he had no reason to believe in deities or unseen hands, but after so much lonesome time passed him by, the retired warrior found himself mumbling a prayer all the same.

Atop the growling mountain, he closed his eyes clad only in the steel leg plates he arrived in. The icy wind was terrible against his bare flesh, but still he prayed. He dreamed and hoped for just one more visitor, one errant pilgrim who remembered his perch up here. He strained his thoughts, pouring his mental being into beseeching a figure whose existence he still doubted, on the barest off-chance that there was weight to this dream and a new day for him to see.

***

"I've never even heard of half of these, dude." Quiet clicking echoed through the apartment as Elroy scrolled through Dan's exhaustive list of computer games. He rubbed the back of his neck as he tried to recognize the obscure and eclectic titles collected over the years. "*Darwinia, NightSky...Legends of Pocoro?* What bargain bins are you pullin' these out of?"

"Hey now, don't be hatin' on that last one; it had a great first half," Dan uttered as he removed a beer from the mini-fridge and walked over to the couch near his friend. His apartment was rather small, cluttered with memorabilia from high school exploits and videogame obsessions. Posters of elves in green caps and burly men wielding chainsaw-laden guns were plastered on the walls while assorted figures sat out in the open around a television. "Kinda sucks that it petered out after that point, though. So much potential..." He sat down and opened the bottle, taking a quick swig.

"What happens?" Dan's larger, sunburnt friend rolled the chair around to look at him, eyebrow raised. The reply he received at first didn't amount to much more than a shrug and another swig.

"It starts out *really* strong. You're making your way up this mountain, there's lots of action, some great boss fights, character customization to Hell and back..." Another drink before he set the bottle down on the coffee table, rubbing his eyes in mild frustration, "Then you get to the top, throw the bad guy off in a *cutscene* and the whole thing turns into some sort of...weird advice-giving scenario where you talk to the villagers you saved. I got near the end, but I'm not sure I ever finished it. You get caught in this overblown dialogue tree with some witch, right? Everything gets all dark and dreary, she starts hollering about 'the next hero'...then she leaves, and *that's* where I stopped playing. Didn't really seem like it was gonna improve."

"Ahh, you don't know that, dude. Maybe she was talkin' about a New Game Plus mode or somethin'," Elroy offered as he double-clicked the icon for *Legends of Pocoro*, a small flag with bright green and red in four alternating squares. "Besides, you can't just *not* finish a game unless it's absolutely terrible. If I was forced to beat *Sonic 2006*, you can play through the rest of a couch potato simulator." A single harp's strings sounded in Dan's speakers as the game began booting up. "We've got a little bit before Rob gets over here for *Kart* Night anyway, just boot up your save and give it one more go." Elroy removed himself from the plushy computer chair, motioning to allow Dan one more apathetic look into the world of Pocoro.

***

Cresting rays of sunlight burst out from the horizon as he opened his eyes. Despite whatever fates conspired against him, something was changing for the warrior. He could feel life stirring within his gut, and with a quick glance into the valley he saw people rushing out to praise the light's return. Had his prayer brought back the sun?

"The Great One smiles upon us all!" He roared, blissfully unaware of how generic and dated the statement sounded. A second wind refreshed him, air rushing through his lungs and a gleam shining in his eye.

His gift had returned to this land, damn the woman and her vile words! They were nothing more than the ramblings of a maddened hag, just as he'd expected. A wave of relief washed over him, blotting out worries and silencing the voices of doubt and self-deprecation. He couldn't help but smile, hoping they were gone for good.

The sounds of celebration resonated throughout the valley as the sun continued its rise. He found it hard to focus on anything now, feeling a worldly weight float off his shoulders. It was a stress realized only after it was gone, and with its disappearance he considered it another side-effect of his anticipatory prayer. He felt almost weightless, as if nothing would keep him tethered to the snowy ground his bare feet rested on, not even…

He made a pained attempt to remove his posterior from the slab, but it yielded no more than ever. Despite this sudden change of fortune, he couldn't reverse his decision. His fate was fixed.

While the sun continued along its upward path, he considered again the idea that this *was* his fate, that sitting here was his destiny if only to serve the villagers. They were casting their defenses back down to the valley floor, an act that made him grin, but would that be enough? Would they make the long trek up the mountain to see him, bask in his presence and return to the villages below, having been enlightened? It was possible, he reasoned, but was it something he cared to see through to whatever end existed for him? With a heavy sigh and an arching of his back, he waited with anticipation for someone to visit him.

A ragged boy passed into his view as the sun approached its zenith, clad in scraps of shoddily patched cloth. The child looked terrified to see him, shying away when the unarmed, stripped down warrior beckoned him closer. After some coaxing, the young lad made his way over the remaining pieces of armor scattered about the peak, giving the warrior a moment of pause.

The boy's movements were...precise. Too precise, as if he was being handled by some unseen force. He found that idea rather absurd, but after such a long period of solitary life the warrior wasn't about to turn down any human interaction. "You've walked up this mountain for some reason, child, but you must explain why. I cannot read your mind." He tried to put on an air of friendliness, but in his haggard and unarmored state it didn't seem to impress the boy.

The boy took a hesitant step forward to pick up the discarded, hefty helmet. The steel gave off a dull gleam in the sunlight, but it was enough to put a smile on the boy's face. He took another step, miniature footprints in the crunchy snow appearing in his wake. A careful gesture set the helmet down in front of the warrior's feet, just far enough away to be out of his reach. He was no longer concerned about his own equipment, shrugging it off with a vested interest in this boy. "Please, my boy: too much time has passed since I last held counsel with another person. You must have come here to do something more than move my helmet around."

The next instances of his life flew by too quickly to acknowledge. As the boy opened his mouth to speak the first words he'd heard in some time, a violent shudder overtook the world. The land around him began falling backwards through time, a brilliant white light following the path of a sun setting in reverse. It was bright enough to blind the warrior for a moment and fierce enough to cause him to feel heat within his bones. So sudden was the event that as the light diminished and the sun retreated back beyond the horizon, his stomach lurched with a strength he hadn't expected.

His eyes opened to see the land submerged in the blackest night once more, a handful of stars doing little to illuminate it. The boy's small footprints were replaced by fresh, white powder, and the warrior's helmet was back in its previous resting place as though it had never been moved. Any note of celebration in the valley was absent, and as he looked below the recently disassembled walls were standing tall and bold. The twin voices of doubt and self-deprecation screamed back into life, tittering away at each other in his mind.

With a heavy sigh and an arching of his back, he waited in dejected posture for someone to visit him, prepared to never see another face again. Such was the fate of Danethor the Strong, fearless savior and champion of the mountain, stuck to a bench for all eternity.

A Perfect Apple
Alois Wittwer

It was the second day in her new home when she planted the sapling. It was a small, pitiable thing at first but she would enjoy watching it grow day by day until it finally blossomed into a beautiful apple tree. The fruit was sweet all year round here and she could eat it whenever she wanted. Once grown, the tree would peek out from behind the neighbor's small, wooden house up by the river bank. For a time, it would be a secluded place, and the girl found comfort far away from the hustle and bustle of the village.

Mother had gone to great lengths to warn her of country folk.

"They have no sense of privacy! They come in uninvited and leave your kitchen empty!"

"So? That just means they're comfortable! Have you forgotten what visitors are like?"

"We don't have them in this household for three very good reasons," she flung her hand up in exasperation. "They'll take all your things and never give them back, they'll ask for ridiculous favours, and they're animals with no sense of morals or public civility."

"Mother!"

"'Getting away from it all' does funny things to your mind, dear."

***

Her house was small but, despite the dire living situation, the girl felt a deep sense of satisfaction. She'd paid for all of this out of her own pocket (she'd had no choice, really). No, it didn't have amenities or gas, but as the first result of her newfound independence it held immeasurable value. And the house wasn't *completely* barren. There was a diary and AM/FM radio nestled in two separate corners respectively. The antenna had been snapped off so radio wasn't an option, but she was sure she'd be able to find some old tapes in the village. Much like the tree the girl planted today, her home held unimaginable potential.

Over the next few days, she familiarized herself with her surroundings. Her house was one of four, placed to circle around the others and form a small, paved yard in the center. A notice board stood in the middle of the enclosure but hadn't been used for a long time, frayed around the edges. She knocked on each door. If the girl did have immediate neighbors, no one was home.

She had better luck outside of the square. Most villagers were friendly, some more than others, but she'd done her best not to ruffle anyone's feathers. From what she could gather, no one worked. Poncho, a particularly sociable sort, said he simply sold off the old things he didn't need anymore and lived off the savings. With all the fruit trees around the village, he didn't need to worry about food and could simply live the good life. Everyone could live the good life thanks to the hard work of the local merchant.

The three statues outside the train station remained a mystery to her, however. Placed in front of the crossing, they looked as if they were designed to draw the attention of any visitors or prospective homeowners, carefully sculpted effigies tempting onlookers with dreams of a luxurious new home. One gold, one silver, one bronze, with enough room for a fourth should the need arise, whatever that need was. The statues were carved like monuments but she couldn't recognize who they were supposed to represent.

She visited the lone proprietor of the village and purchased a plain red couch that just barely fit inside her home and a pink vanity the owner described as "simply lovely." The vanity was for Poncho who seemed obsessed with exercising but didn't have any way to look at himself in his home. Her mother collected furniture like this—old mirrors, brass, reflective surfaces. Abrasive. She didn't want this anywhere near her.

Now she understood why the furniture was so cheap: the customer was expected to carry all goods to their home themselves, no concerns about health and safety, and some items looked unmistakably second-hand. By the time she'd visited Poncho and arrived home, daylight was already fading. Curled up on the couch, the wrinkles of the fabric printed like age onto her skin. Abrasive wasn't a good word to describe her mother.

***

It was Poncho who first suggested she take up morning aerobics to iron out the creases built up from daily training. She wasn't quite sure what he meant but relished the opportunity to start the day early with communal exercise, huddled around the town's local water fountain with friends. A different kind of ritual from what she was used to.

But familiarity persisted. The villagers had, alongside their boastfulness, a tendency to loan things and quickly forget who had them originally. *Who haa saia that to her?* At times, the girl felt like little more than a slave forced to do her master's bidding, ferrying knickknacks back and forth between folks, but most of the time she cared for the villagers as if they were her own children. They were a forgetful bunch, having lived so long in a village that promoted a lack of productivity, so it felt natural that they would gravitate towards the outsider for direction. She didn't want to deal with that pressure tonight. She moved here to get away from this incessant need.

Her Saturday nights were typically spent down by the seashore, fishing for the biggest catch. This was *the* activity to make a fortune and the heavy rain tonight could coax even the rarest fish out of hiding. A few hours spent fishing each night and you'd never have to worry about money again. Now, she could buy whatever she wanted *ana* renovate her tiny home. It was a welcomed change after living so long in a cramped apartment with her mother. She could never make this sort of money living in the city.

She wouldn't visit the beach tonight, though. Instead she walked through the orchard of orange trees she had planted earlier that week. One of her closest friends in the village, Mitzi, had given her a leftover orange she had lying about as thanks for finding her handkerchief. The girl had never seen an orange in the village before and promptly scattered the seeds across an acre with the hope that they would grow. At first she was worried the saplings didn't have enough water; it had been so hot during the week and she had no way to care for them. But the trees had sprung to life in a lovely criss-cross pattern. It was a bit difficult finding a pathway so late at night, though, even with the soft glow of the moonlight off the oranges, so the girl took a cursory glance over her handiwork and headed back home. Much like everything else she did in the village, the orchard was for herself more than the villagers and besides, they would get lost mos—no, she didn't want to think about them tonight.

As she was walking home, she heard a soft, lilting tune off in the distance, distinct from the gentle pitter-patter of rain on the ground. A funny-looking man sat perched on a little box strumming a guitar under the roof of the train station. He was soaked to the bone, a sad slouch. He played on regardless, to an audience of no one, with a grin that betrayed his tenacity.

He looked up as she approached, resting the guitar on his lap, and told her stories that felt like they came from a book. He was a solitary musician who travelled from town to town playing music to fresh faces each and every night. His music was free and for the people, no fat cats allowed. He seemed to find it fulfilling.

It was midnight when he stopped playing; she stayed the whole night. When she got back home, she found a recording was resting in her pocket. The cassette player snapped open with an urgency common to analog devices, and the girl gently placed the tape inside the cradle and eased it shut. It didn't sound the same—recordings never do—and the speaker was broken.

She was dazzled at how anyone could live like that. Wouldn't it get lonely playing to passing strangers each night with no place to call home? Maybe this was how people were supposed to be like? Her mother didn't have anyone else in her life. Why did she say such horrible things to her? She sat down on the squeaky floorboards until the tape clicked off. She hit rewind and played the song again.

***

The letter arrived in December:

Dear Valentine,
I was thinking about you as I had my morning coffee. Do you remember when you were little, and I gave you a sip? You didn't sleep for days! That was a bad idea.
Live and learn.
Mom.

Her hands froze to the sides of the paper, holding on in the biting cold as she read the message over and over again. This had to be a joke. Who would do this?

Valentine stumbled over to the train station and sat down on the nearest bench, waiting for the next train to come by. She'd get on the next one and leave this place, forever. She didn't care how long she had to wait. She wasn't welcome here. Why did she ever think otherwise?

Hunched over the bench, she held on like death. Valentine waited the whole day; the train never came. The town bell tolled as the hours slowly passed. A small jade monument, just like all of the other statues, had joined the others now in front of the station. The snow fell like ash, hiding its features, blurring her vision, but it was there all the same. The statue was a permanent celebration for everyone who had transformed their small home into a mansion. Valentine had been the last, and it was smaller than the others. She rubbed her eyes with her fingers and, no, it couldn't be her. But it looked like all the others. The same dress and pointy hat, the same exuberant expression, smaller now, unimportant. The statues were all the same. It was just a coincidence this one had been made, right?

The crossing remained still. Nothing more than a decoration. Perhaps a train would come by someday, Valentine thought, and it would be her hearse.

***

The cicadas were singing when Valentine came back. Poncho had left and the goodbye letter he sent to her was a trivial afterthought. She wasn't even sure who actually wrote them anymore. Valentine would have liked to say goodbye to him, though. Despite her distrust of the villagers, Poncho had been good to her. She didn't begrudge him for wanting to find something exciting in his life again. No, she was hurt that her friendship had meant nothing to him.

A grumpy man called Murphy moved into Poncho's lot. He seemed genuinely unhappy to be here. She enjoyed his blithe comments and condescending attitude so much that she made herself uncomfortable.

Valentine couldn't go back to the routine she'd established before. Nothing felt genuine anymore. Once-concerted efforts to donate all the fossils she found buried underground to the local museum slackened. Where were these things even coming from? Maybe the person who knew could also tell her how her house was renovated while she was asleep.

In her wandering to while away the hours of the afternoon, she stumbled upon the old apple tree she'd planted so long ago. It still stood as proudly as before, bearing the same perfect fruit exactly like the moment it first bloomed. Except now the fruit held no finer meaning to her. It was a bland, chewy thing that turned her stomach. As she picked up the leftover fruit off the ground, she realized that this tree would be brimming with apples again within a few days. It would always be producing something. It would never stop.

And the seasons would come and go like always. The years would go by. The salmon would swim upstream for March and the fireflies would illuminate the night sky each June. Halloween, Christmas, and New Years would come and go with crushing mundanity. The villagers would go about the same celebrations. They would leave whenever they felt like it for whatever reason they desired on a train that never materialized, like ghosts.

Except for Valentine.

Valentine had exhausted herself by caring for a village that gave her nothing back. And what had she really done for herself?

She rummaged through her belongings at home; the collection of junk she'd amassed ever since she moved in, searching in vain for something to comfort her. Her house had turned into a museum, filled with collectibles she received for special holidays she'd attended throughout the years. Valentine had nothing that suggested a person lived here. She'd long since gotten rid of her bed to fit in an oversized boxing ring. She didn't need to sleep. When had she last slept?

When had she moved in?

Valentine struggled to remember. No one else would remember. She didn't know anyone else.

She rushed out into the village, desperate to find somebody she could reminisce with. But Poncho and Mitzi had long since moved out of the village. The older villagers that were here when Valentine first moved in had never spent as much time with her, so wrapped up in their own comings and goings. She was a stranger now and, far from finding it invigorating, she was violently alone.

The girl wandered down to the beach and peered out into the inky blackness. She stood in a stillness that could last forever. Were you so sure of yourself, mother? When was the last time she told her she loved her? Valentine had never done something so simple. Why did it matter so much? She just loved a memory now, an empty face.

Murphy walked over to Valentine to wish her a happy birthday. He wanted to be the first. He couldn't sleep.

"How old are you today?"

Valentine paused. Murphy laughed and shrugged off her uncertainty as embarrassment. He knew he wasn't *supposed* to ask that question. Valentine wasn't embarrassed, though. She honestly couldn't remember how long she'd been here or even where she came from. The uncomfortable silence divided the pair and Murphy made a hasty retreat, gruffly muttering about some furniture he had to buy in the morning. The waves crashed against Valentine's feet and soaked her shoes.

What was she afraid of now? She didn't need to be polite anymore. She didn't have anything to lose.

Valentine returned to the town square, her familiar home surrounded by three strange ones. She knocked on the doors of her neighbors but this time she didn't wait for an answer. She went inside each house that had ignored her and found immaculate, two-storey homes furnished with stunning furniture and things she'd never seen in the village before. But nothing was out of the ordinary except for the complete lack of any living person. Cockroaches scurried across floors so clean Valentine could eat breakfast off of them. The three houses she'd considered empty had been inhabited—should have been inhabited—but Valentine had never seen anyone else like her in the village before.

Deep in the basement of the last house, Valentine spotted a vanity stuffed awkwardly into a corner, forgotten just like the rest of the homes, spotless, a familiar face reflected back at the girl. The same face frozen in the bust of the statues outside the train station, a happiness with no focus, a happiness stuck in place for eternity.

***

Valentine had forgotten about the shimmering cherry blossoms that littered the sky each April. She never had to plan for this unexplained event each year that painted the entire town in a luminous pink, when the trees dropped petals that looked like watercolor paintings melting in the harsh summer heat. The four statues framed in perfect unison in front of the train station flowers that had refused to wilt despite all the time that passed.

The village was never like this, originally. Valentine had done this but she couldn't remember doing it. Now all sorts of fruits lined the acres in meticulously organized orchards. Flowers, maps, and signposts had been erected to guide any would-be visitors to all of the town's highlights. Poncho and Mitzi had seen this village grow from nothing to a magnificent utopia, and they'd learnt all they could from living here before moving on with their lives. The new villagers, so unfamiliar yet so friendly, shared the same enthusiastic cheer and forgetfulness of Valentine's older companions. Time had changed this forgotten, useless, uncaring village into something wonderful.

And up by the river bank, behind the neighbor's small, wooden house, the apple tree stood proudly, bearing fruit no matter the season. Perfect. A monument to the hours wasted waiting.

But Valentine was the same.

She was the same.

See You on the Other Side
Shelley Du

A jolt shoots through Saphira. She's teleported to the same place. The pre-boss-battle cutscene plays out like sleep paralysis, suffocating but lucid.

Bam.

Here comes the mini-boss, Kylin, a thing too grotesque for its own pay scale. Oh look, its minion wolfies, too. In another incarnation not that long ago, Saphira's party, Surge, had already handed over their lives multiple times here.

Now that their Thief, Caime, has triggered the battle again, the train has left the station. Nowhere to go but though an abominable cutscene, and then things will really get ugly.

She knows it's not Caime's fault. The trigger has been tested many times to make sure that when Caime hits the trigger, the same cutscene has to play—Arrow Acorn Studio takes pride in its polished code. Maybe Saphira should be grateful. At least her feet have never randomly done the Ragdoll Dance and her head has never been stuck halfway between the game world and untextured limbo.

Small miracles.

***

The background music changes to a grandiose organ piece. Saphira jumps backwards reflexively; her flailing hand almost clipping Mason the Mage's ear. She's positioned so close to Kylin's minions that she could reach over with a marker and draw moustaches on their faces.

The mandatory pep talk from Nivan and Caime confirm her fear. It's not about what they say; the only time they can ever speak is when they regurgitate the script. What concerns Saphira is where they say it.

The Holy Highness of Failure, their almighty controller better known as Pea-Brain, learned nothing from the last defeat. Yet again, Surge charges into battle with two undefended magic users on the frontline and physical attackers in the back.

Saphira and Mason's eyes lock. Not a hint of shock from Mason, just his perpetual sadness. Justified, maybe, but it still kills Saphira inside to see him like that. She never knows if he's going to have the energy to be momentarily un-sad again, or if he's fixed in this state for eternity.

The battle begins. Caime receives the first command. Must be nice to be the speediest of the group, Surge's guinea pig.

Skill: Steal.

Target: Wolf A.

The command seals her movement and her target. Caime rushes to her target shifting sideways moments before they collide, swiping at the wolf. She rips off a handful of soggy fur, out of which they might be able to craft something. Wooly hat. Carpet. If they can find a good blacksmith, they can make a Rookie Sword.

Why waste an early turn for a patch of mud-soaked animal hair? Surely if they were going to loot something, Kylin's rare possessions would make far more sense. Oh wait, Pea-Brain. That's why.

The next command comes to Saphira.

Skip Turn.

Sometimes Saphira wonders if Pea-Brain uses the menus by chewing on the controller. No one needs healing right now, but a Skip Turn robs Saphira of the opportunity to use Defend.

It's Wolf A's turn now, and it looks rather unhappy with its bald patch, blood oozing down its side. It growls at Caime, perhaps wanting a pawful of scalp in return. However, its movements are as rigidly defined as Surge's, and it is predetermined to go after the weakest link. As the only person with Defence stats in the single digits, it sucks to be Saphira right now.

Bracing herself is out of the question. She missed that train when she skipped the turn. Saphira tries to evade to the side, like Caime would. Pity Dexterity isn't her forte either—Saphira's foot catches on a branch and she trips.

Wolf A sinks its fangs into her forearm. It feels like she's caught in bear trap: electric pain bursts up her shoulder as her bones meet its teeth. She stumbles backwards, rolling on landing to minimize the impact.

The good news is that her spine is undamaged, still counting for the "Almost New" category if she wants to sell it to an organ trader. Wolf A hangs onto her, crashing with Saphira and smashing its head into a rock. Wolves' heads are hard as granite, but the impact catches it by surprise.

Saphira is not a physical combatant, but this is the perfect opportunity for someone who is. Say, Nivan, the Warrior.

Physical attack: Yes.

Target Wolf: YES.

Target Wolf B: NO!

Nivan mouths "I'm sorry" as he dashes past Saphira. She's on her own now. Wolf A is still firmly attached to her, and while it's impossible to get used to the feeling of being shredded, she begins to notice how tiring it is to have 130 pounds of dead weight clamped onto her arm. It doesn't help that she's as strong and durable as wet toilet paper.

She tries to poke Wolf A in the eye with her staff, only to be repelled mere molecules away before landing the strike. Too close to the Attack command she's not given. The only self-defence she can improvise is flapping around Wolf A, hoping that a fleck of dust knocks it out.

Meanwhile, whatever Nivan did, it worked. Wolf B howls, sporting a new gash on its forehead. Its glare fixes upon Saphira. Not something she can take personally; she'd attack herself too if she were the wolf.

Saphira's neck feels ablaze as warm liquid rains down her torso. Yet she remains conscious. She is streaming blood rather than squirting it: a missed artery is a missed critical hit. Small miracles.

Even luckier for Saphira is Wolf B's failure to grab onto her in the way the hanging Wolf A did. The Goddess of Probability must've smiled. She could last until the next ally's turn. A Healing Potion and she's good, stickier and redder, but good.

It's Mason's turn. As long as he tosses her a potion, Saphira might still have some fight in her.

Physical Attack.

Had this mistake been forced upon any other, they would've been visibly frustrated, but the slouching Mason just pulls out his tome. Saphira expects Pea-Brain to mess up with full-throttle creativity, but she's still caught off guard by Mason's assigned target.

Target: Saphira.

She hears the thud of his tome colliding with her head before feeling it. Mason is as weak of a physical attacker as she is. If Saphira isn't already doing her part in their interspecies luncheon, it would've hurt the tome more than her.
But right now, that is enough to deplete the last of her HP.
Her chest tightens as her breath ties itself into a knot. A sharp pain in her neck. A sweet muddy taste. Crunching of the bridge of her nose. An explosion of light specks appearing in back of her eyes. A buzzing in her ears. The fading of the buzzing in her ears. The fading of everything in general.

***

Saphira wakes up and runs her tongue across her teeth instinctively. Her wounds have been erased, yet the hurt lingers.
This is what happens after a Game Over. The reload provides the illusion of a clean slate, but doesn't fully wash away what has already happened. Surge remembers, their bodies remember. Saphira's chest still pulsates with a hot, stabbing pain, as if she inhaled a fish hook. Her arms still feel like they're filled with broken glass, but any sign of injury has vanished.
Over the course of the journey, her body parts have been hacked off, re-grown, immolated, re-grown, shredded, and re-grown again. She doesn't know how many limbs she's gone though anymore, her sensations overloaded beyond recognition. She could have a look, but that would involve pulling through layers of tunic

and dress. Pea-Brain says she has to dress like a filo parcel with bells and ribbons. Pea-Brain's wish is her command.

In a moment, Surge will regroup. They will charge head first into the same fight, prefaced once again with the same convoluted speech about fate and heroes. Saphira remembers her lines well: how they are not bound by fate and they just needed to believe in themselves, as if any of them would choose to catapult themselves into another suicide mission.

She's Surge's sole Healer, the typecast "Soft-Spoken Holy Maiden with a Heart of Gold." Saphira doesn't know if she actually is soft-spoken, since no one here can actually speak. They can beep pre-set texts in boxes hanging over their heads, each sentence just about personal as a list of terms and conditions.

***

A familiar flash, and the world momentarily freezes around her. In Saphira's peripheral vision, she sees Nivan frantically scribbling on the ground. His attempt to speak out is desperate: there's always a chance they'll all die again before anyone gets to read his message, and the dirt will be wiped back to its factory-fresh state.

They call this "Morphing," when the world freezes still, and Surge's clothing, weapons and accessories shift into something else. Sometimes Pea-Brain gives a Healing Potion to an injured member. Sometimes Pea-Brain's even generous enough to give them two. Though, that's not why they love Morphing. Morphing is when Surge has a brief shot at real communication: they still can't speak freely, but they can move. They scribble down their messages on whatever they can get their hands on, releasing their thoughts, absorbing others.

All of the party participates, except for Mason. He goes straight for the grog. Maybe it's easier to carve on the ground with staffs, swords and daggers, and Mason just has the luck to be assigned with pillow-sized tomes as weapons. Perhaps he just prefers diesel-scented alcohol over Faith, Friendship and Fondness or whatever other corny platitudes that start with the letter F. Saphira can't blame him.

***

It depends on Pea-Brain's mood. Morphing could take anywhere from seconds to hours. She affects a mournful laugh watching Nivan flailing to scribble, either oblivious to the likely futility or in denial about it. That's their Warrior, alright.

He should've been the Holy Maiden; too bad that it's just not the done thing. Nivan is the designated hero, Pea-Brain's avatar who is to lead Surge across the world and save them all. Nivan really tries to live up to his role, eager with morning sunlight shining out of every orifice. He always says the right lines at the right time, the texts scroll too fast, beeps pitched too high. He trembles with every scratchy motivational line, fooling no one but himself.

Their hero's way out of his depth. That makes four of them, but things are harder on Nivan. He may come off as a bit naive, but his memory is unparalleled—he absorbs everything. She sees the way he glances at roadside flowers on the journey. That's where his heart really lies: appreciating little things and basking in the joy of discovery instead of playing savior with painted-on earnestness, stuffing his head with cyclical death memories.

Saphira has had plenty of opportunities to get to know Nivan; supposedly she's his soulmate. There are enough cutscenes with longing gazes into each other's eyes to fuel a thousand dating spam ads.

The Forest of Bells arc had been an utter mess: two sixteen-year-olds united by nothing but an arranged marriage is as awkward as one could possibly imagine. Now, at least half of the scripted events involve being physically way too close for both of their comfort, and while she's stuck there, she has to endure Nivan's leathery armor. That thing stinks with the fermented bodily fluids of every slain creature in a thirty-mile radius.

Though the script declared, "I belong to you, you belong to me," Nivan belongs to no one. He belongs *with* someone, just not her. When Nivan and Saphira's flower of romance was peeled to forced-bloom, Mason went from garden-variety mopey to clinically depressed.

As far as Saphira's concerned, they deserve each other way more than she and Nivan do, and it would be a favor to all concerned. So what if Nivan is so sunny that it hurt? So what if a good day for Mason is a day not catatonic under a tree root?

At least Saphira had one honest conversation with Nivan in the Forest, not as lovers but as fellow prisoners. After Nivan tied a Buttercup Bell onto her braid, a Morphing happened. Nivan grabbed her by the sleeve, more urgently than he'd ever done before. He looked terrified.

"You're handling it well," Nivan wrote. "How? I can't be that nonchalant. I don't want to die."

"Sucks when we do," Saphira agreed.

"No, I mean, I wanna keep on living."

"This isn't living."

"I don't want to permanently disappear before I've lived to see it through."

"It's not that big a deal. We always get reloaded. We'll live."

"Don't you get it?" Nivan wanted to speak, but only managed grunts. "If Pea-Brain gives up, we will die permanently. Every time we reload, he's that much closer to quitting."

He stared right through Saphira, writing down his words with so much force his blade bent.

"I'm scared, Saphira."

***

Saphira seeks Caime first, finding her curled up near a cherry tree; alert, shaky but consciously trying not to move. Her wide-open eyes tremble in hyperawareness. She looks like an architect's proudest work, abandoned and left to decay for decades and now comically buried in pink petals. Not that the heroes truly look bad, in a conventional sense. Surge has their own eloquently crafted outfits, while everyone else in this world is stuck with one of the seven generic templates. Saphira knows they are created to be beautiful for Pea-Brain. Eternally beautiful, like the preserved nuclear shadows long after an explosion.

Surge drags around more than twelve of each clothing set, yet Caime is only given ridiculously short shorts and a belt for a bra. Pea-Brains need sex appeal. Sexy bare midriff. Sexy bare ribs. Sexy skin shivering in the melting snow.

Caime slowly stretches out her arm, trembling. With the cautiousness of a card-tower architect, Caime picks up a branch. Normally, Caime is too highly-strung to move this slowly and deliberately. Her combined Speed and Spirit stats close in on 200, making her practically immune to sleep, and that is without taking into account that Pea-Brain has an obsession with feeding her stimulating potions.

Although it takes forever, the Thief insists on writing everything clearly: no shorthand, no cursive, and proper capitalization: "I wish I could just tell you all to run. Fuck off back to your Healer cloister or mother-of-pearl palace or wherever you lived. Fuck off and never see me again. We all know that our ~~fate~~...that ~~our~~ lives are cemented together. You can jump off the edge of the world, but if I so much as wiggle my fucking toe the wrong way we'll just reload to do it all again." Caime finished with a drawing of a heart, symmetrical and genuine.

***

Caime was the last to join Surge, the mandatory cupcake cute girl. During their first Morphing all together, no one was prepared for how much she swore. Saphira has no memories of the life before the script. Maybe her vocabulary used to be as limited, had she ever been fourteen.

"I can't believe the crap that comes out of your textbox, you smug wanker. 'All we need is the love to light our way to our miracle.' Really? Why don't you just cross over the screen and print yourself on Pea-Brain's hug pillow if you love him so much, you stuck-up shitbag," was the first unscripted thing Caime ever communicated to Saphira.

She was more amused than upset, "You think I would insult my intelligence and yours with that line of my own free will? If I had my way, I'd say we need a waterproof tent long before we need Lock of Trust. I'm basically carrying a brick in my pocket here."

"Wait, so you don't mean your lines?" Caime was taken aback.

"You do?"

"I'm the comedy relief, remember? Hell, like I'm getting any lines relevant enough for me to feel anything. I kinda space out. You know, let the textbox do its thing while I gaze into the sky. Are you telling me I actually say shit like that?!"

"Not yet. But when it happens, I'll tattoo it on my forearm and shove it in your face everyday until I inevitably have to sacrifice myself for the greater good." Saphira drew a wink at the end. Caime stared at Saphira for a moment, before bursting out in silent laughter.

***

Caime no longer laughs. She no longer expresses much at all. "I just want this to stop. I'm so tired I've forgotten how to cry." Caime always stared, but there's something especially empty about it today.

"I haven't rested since I joined. My mind is spinning. I'm dreaming and I'm awake. I'm alert and I'm dead and I can't go on anymore. I am exhausted and I can't go on anymore."

Saphira wonders what Pea-Brain would think of their suffering. Probably that their pseudo-deaths are disposable, easily overwritten. So what if Surge's deaths are temporary? The pain doesn't dwindle because they already lived through it in multiple past lives. It's like Pea-Brain repeatedly pulling their nails for fun.

"Saphira. Make this stop. Please." The Caime Saphira used to know would never plead. Caime's dead. What is forced to live on is her corpse manipulated into whatever state that pleases Pea-Brain's fleeting fancies. Caime lifts up her branch and tries to continue writing, only to explode into violent retching. The cutscene snaps alive before her vomit hits the floor.

***

Kylin's battle theme blares again. To Saphira's relief, she is now away from the enemy line by quite a stretch. Seems Pea-Brain has finally learned something from the past three defeats and shields the low-Defence members at the back. Along with the...stronger Defenders? Good job, Pea-Brain, now everyone is in the same back row.

Caime's move. Pea-Brain tries something different this time.

Skill: Item.

Item: Speed-Acc Potion.

Target: Caime.

The formation tradeoff is that whoever goes in front gets twice the Speed but half the Defence. With Caime in the back, their main agility specialist loses her advantage. Pea-Brain compensates for the lowered Speed with Items. A Speed-Acc raises Speed by ten points. The effect stacks, so Pea-Brain loves forcing the potions down their throats. Saphira likes the taste of Speed-Acc even though she's rarely given it. Caime describes it as seagull shit fermented in a barrel of liquid vitamins. Either way, Caime has already drunk enough for her teeth to chatter on the rim of the glass bottles.

It's Saphira's turn. Holding onto the staff counts as touching wood. Just as long as it's not Skip Turn again.

Physical Attack.

Target: Wolf A.

She whacks Wolf A on the flank. The staff springs right back, as a numbing vibration runs up her arms and stuns her shoulder blades. *Hurts me more than it hurts you, Wolf A.* Saphira will still feel the whiplash on her arms if she survives until the next turn. She hasn't broken a single lustrous wolf hair.

Wolf A doesn't give Saphira a second glance: it sinks its fangs into Mason's knee. He lets out a bloodcurdling howl. When Surge screams, it is the only time they get to hear each other's voices. Saphira expects Mason's to be hoarse, like he gargled gravel every morning. Instead, she's always surprised at how high-pitched he is.

Nivan's next move is disturbingly reasonable.

Item: Healing Potion.

Target: Mason.

Pea-Brain seems to be learning. The warm fuzzies Mason anticipate from Nivan evaporate the moment they hear the distinct error beep: they are out of Healing Potions. Nivan's turn is wasted. The Baton of Pain is passed to Wolf B now. It takes a full minute before lunging at Caime, only to miss as Caime evades its attack. All things considered, Caime is still as quick as ever.

Wolf A returns to its position. There are mere specks of blood on Mason's robe, but the damage is clear. He tries to stand up and fails. No wonder, his leg is the shape of a curly fry. Tough, there's no sick leave or disability pension for heroes. Mason has work to do.

Skill: Fireball.

Target: Kylin.

If Mason has an opinion, he's not showing it. He does what he does best, casting an ineffective spell with as much professional pride as a goat shitting off a cliff.

Fire elementals look aggressive and powerful, but using fire against a wind elemental? There should be a special Hell for people this vain. To a very trained eye, the only hint of damage on Kylin is a singed whisker, who prepares to unleash Wind Bind. Saphira bets the largest gemstone on her staff that Pea-Brain thinks "gentler" elementals like wind are reserved for styling hair.

Wind Bind creates a vortex around Nivan. Its immaculate programming leaves enough downward draft that pins him to the ground. Sand particles buffet Nivan, adding new lacerations by the second. But that's nothing compared to the force of the air around him forming a compression tunnel so he can't breathe. Wind Bind isn't going to subside anytime soon. He's on the way out and he knows it.

***

Nivan's a simple, young man, with one simple facial expression no matter the terror. For a moment, Saphira feels like she's back in Forest of Bells with him.

That's when she has an idea.

The hit rate is a curious thing. The otherwise watertight system has one flaw—it cannot truly generate accuracy randomly. Instead, the law decides the upper and lower limits, and anything in between is in Surge's tiny amount of control.

Saphira's healing spells have a hit rate of 86.4% to 94.9%: if she tries her best to hit, she will heal 94% of the time. For all the scripting and programming, manipulating the probability is within her reach.

Small miracles.

It felt as trivial as a consolation plastic toy in a treasure chest until now. She will try harder than she ever has. She's going for the 86.4%.

Pea-Brain gives Saphira the command to heal every turn. She aims anywhere and everywhere that isn't her allies. She can't help but spill some healing on Surge, but if she's lucky, they will not stay alive. One by one, her party falls. They writhe and struggle like crushed worms, but it won't be long. It won't be long.

I'm sorry. Saphira misses. *This is it, Mason. I thought we would have an eternity together and I would get to know you one day: I guess I should've taken the initiative.*

Saphira misses again. *Sorry, Nivan. I know you wanted to live on, but I need to put a stop to this. You deserve to have a life, not a joke.*

We don't have to keep on suffering like this. Saphira misses again. *Goodnight, Caime. I hope you don't dream, but have the deepest, most peaceful sleep.*

It takes forever, but she's the last one standing. Among the mangled bodies, Saphira's resolve is absolute. Missing herself with her healing spells takes more skill than ever, and with the injuries adding up it becomes harder and harder to pull it off.

But she's diligent and a damn good Healer. She always has been.

I don't believe in another life. But if there is such a thing, I hope it's better than this one. If fate demands our souls are intertwined, let's defy fate by never crossing paths. Let's never see each other on the other side.

Patched Up
Ryan Morning

Drakeguy
Project Lead

Many of you have reported that Coster the Grenadier's "Apex" ability, Bombardment, is not calculating damage per its in-game description: it is currently *adding* 60% to projectile damage instead of reducing it to that amount.

We're aware of the problem, and we intend to address it as soon as possible.

***

It was the lack of recrimination. Somehow the way the entire faction took the news made him feel as if they'd always known that he was a fraud, that he was only popular because of a glitch, that he was destined to be rejected from tournament play. He could've taken anger, but pity brought him low.

Raya the Blade and Kamen the Skirmisher were out of their comfort zone. Stone-faced even by the standards of a character whose in-game emotional spectrum ran from good-natured determination to grim determination, Coster glowered at his uneaten meal and brooded.

"What Kamen meant to say," Raya said sharply, "was your *other* abilities are good, even though you didn't have to use them."

"Exactly!" Kamen beamed, plucked from the hole he'd been so enthusiastically digging. "The Anti-Armor thing. See, for Raya and me, armor is one of our counters. We can't do much to it."

"Put it this way," said Coster. "Your Double Tap sees a lot of use, doesn't it?"

"It's sort of my staple, yeah," said Kamen, sipping his drink.

"Whereas I've gone entire matches without Anti-Armor being used. Without anyone even investing character points in it. For the time it takes to deploy, I could be dealing damage."

"Well, uh…"

"It's a situational ability for a situation that never arises. *Your* second ability is an instantaneous shot that deals bonus damage and always hits, mine is a ponderous pseudo-tactical timewaster that leaves me wide open for half a year."

"Now hang on," Raya protested, "earlier you were saying this was a team game. So many abilities interlink, work off of each other."

"Raya, you can take anyone apart up close. You practically go it solo. Kamen runs around harassing the opposition and then falls back if it gets too hot."

Kamen shrugged and took another drink, as if to say, yeah, that's how I roll.

"Me?" Coster sighed. "I lob grenades at the mobs. And I was fine with that, it was how I worked. But late game? By late game I'd unlocked Bombardment, and I wasn't on the sidelines anymore. I called the shots. Literally! A volley of grenades right into the middle of the enemy and then everyone else would mop up."

Coster reached below his seat and brought out his grenade launcher. Like everything else in the game, it was comically oversized: there was no way of mistaking it for any other weapon, even when viewed from a distance.

"I'd figured out how it all worked. I was used to it, happy with it. On the bad days, when my player was new or maybe unlucky or Hell, even just plain lousy at the game, I coped. Because I knew how it would work on the good days."

He dropped the launcher. The table sagged and the crockery rattled.

"What'll happen now? I checked out the numbers. If they tweak it, Bombardment's effectiveness will be halved. Worse than halved. And even now it's not a win button! Sometimes the enemy is just too tough, there are too many of them, and they mow through us even after I soften them up. So if the devs make it worse than that, where do I fit in? What do I actually *do*?"

"You'll still be in the roster," Raya said gently. "You're one of the original characters. People will always play you."

"Right," Kamen agreed, "you were in the launch trailer and everything."

"I don't know if I want that. I think I'd sooner be forgotten than be "that guy," the one only the delusional newbies play because they just don't understand how bad I am." Coster sunk onto the table. "Becoming a handicap for old hands that deliberately pick a shitty character to show how great they are—"

"Oh," someone interrupted, "am I missing your pity party? I'm upset that I wasn't sent an invitation."

"I tried," Raya said automatically, "but the computer insisted that smarmy@jackass wasn't a real email address."

"Beat it, Meraclus," said Kamen.

Coster looked up. Meraclus definitely looked the part of a smarmy jackass. Something sort of chiselled about the face, likely a rip-off of a star from a particular kind of action movie: glowing eyes, a high-collared overcoat, and a sword that loomed on the back like a surfboard. It was all so clichéd that it made Coster, a tall gruff weapons expert with a cheek scar, shudder at how much worse his design could've been.

"I just thought I'd come by," Meraclus continued, all smiles, "and help console the cheater."

"Oh, screw you," Kamen stiffened, and would have stood up if Coster hadn't placed a hand on his shoulder.

"Please, like he didn't know something was amiss." Meraclus smirked. He leaned towards Coster. "Newsflash: if one of your grenades can't take out a siege tank with one shot, didn't it make you suspicious when an apparently *weakened* grenade managed to do it?"

"You're not big, and you're not clever," said Kamen. "Back off. I sure as Hell know that you don't come out on top when we fight."

Meraclus didn't change his expression. Coster realized that the smirk must have been his face's default, at-rest appearance; what a thing for a modeller to do to their creation. God knew how that'd affect a personality.

"I rather think I am big and clever, actually. I have higher attribute scores than you. You only ever beat me because you're always running around, too scared to face me."

"What an incredible comeback," said Raya. "He only beats you, repeatedly, because he's faster and more skilled and refuses to fight on your terms. Wow. How can he hear that one without being burned to cinders."

"How very mature."

Coster had had enough. He got the feeling that Meraclus was the type to assume that silence wasn't being the bigger man. He likely saw a refusal to engage as cowardice, and right now Coster agreed.

"Says the man who brings up martial performance and then regrets it because being reminded of his failure hurts his feelings," Coster clapped, but briefly, because that sort of thing annoyed him. "Well done, I'm now acutely aware of how terrible a character I am, so please quit embarrassing yourself."

Meraclus strode off, aloof and triumphant, although no one in the canteen appeared impressed or otherwise moved by the confrontation.

"Don't mind that oaf." Raya watched him swagger off. "They added Merac in v1.6; yet another sword swinger, one of those try-hards that thinks that because the in-game fiction portrays him as a badass, he's actually a badass."

"Didn't even have any food with him," Kamen said disgustedly. "Came here looking to poke fun at the veteran. What a joke."

"He's right, though," Coster sighed. "It's cheating. Straight-up cheating."

"Come on! *You* didn't know."

"You know what he's like. You shouldn't let him get to you," Raya insisted.

"He doesn't, don't worry. But it's nothing I haven't told myself. A bunch of my players knew about it, I'm sure of it, and that doesn't reflect well on me. Especially when they insist that if it's in-game, the devs must have meant for it to happen."

"Like anyone's ever cared about the natural order of things."

"It's like, uh, an athlete being slipped steroids by someone else," said Kamen. "Not their fault, when you think about—"

"Not the best example," Raya interjected.

"I imagine the average athlete would notice it when they grew unexpected muscles," said Coster. "No. On some level I *must* have known about it. I deserve to be nerfed, it happens to other people all the time. I'm just too damn selfish to take it."

"Forgetting silly hypotheticals for now," Raya continued, with a meaningful glance at Kamen, "you shouldn't be so quick to admit defeat."

"How d'you mean?"

"She means, sure, things will change," Kamen explained, "but who's to say they'll be totally insurmountable?"

"Indeed," Raya agreed, "it's all very well to be gracious about the hand you're dealt but there's little point in speculating about the deck."

After a moment of silence Coster replied, "I'm not sure that metaphor works."

"Sorry," Raya shrugged. "I threw everything at the wall to see what would stick."

"The entire *franchise* loves to do that," Kamen exclaimed brightly. He currently had a sheathed katana and an 1800s S&W revolver on his hip. "If I hadn't seen how the players reacted, I'd never have realized that it's a little weird to have knights fighting cowboys fighting wizards fighting robots."

"I never did understand whether my "people" are a nation state or an alien species," Coster mused. "Perhaps I'm just a human who happens to be a sort of fluorescent blue color."

"I wouldn't try to figure out the devs' motives," Raya glowered. "Lots of insensitivity and cultural appropriation."

"You do go on about that a lot," Kamen said, a tad reproachfully.

"I'm an Indian woman who keeps spouting Korean idioms, I dual-wield sais, and for some reason this tattoo on my face is a Chinese hanzi."

"Ah. Well. Point taken."

"They haven't even given you a mask," she continued, "so I can't say I get the logic behind calling you Kamen. Unless it's a metaphor."

"Why would I have a mask?"

Raya saw that Kamen was serious, and shrugged. "Never mind."

Coster had a joyless spoonful of whatever the pabulum in his bowl was meant to be.

"So," said Kamen, not a character used to silence, "what's the tattoo say in Chinese?"

"In my bio, the developers claim it means 'swiftness'," Raya explained. "But according to a bunch of people on the official forums, it actually means 'feet.' More or less."

Coster grimaced. He could imagine the nicknames that'd come from that. Sometimes, if they were really popular, the devs themselves embraced them.

"Maybe they'll sneak in a change to your texture," he hazarded.

"Even though it was reported four versions ago, Kamen's head still turns invisible when you view him from behind. I'm not getting my hopes up."

"Hey, I'm part Spostarite, and we're genetically engineered to appear transparent from certain angles. It aids stealth..."

"There we go again," Raya said bitterly. "Don't fix things, just try and work with them. Flavor your flaws and they add character. People will fight tooth and nail to defend what's there, just because it's there."

Except for me, Coster thought. *I'm broken by merit of being too good. Now the truth is out, now everyone hated me all along and they shout down anyone who says otherwise. And they're right to do it.*

***

Coster emerged into the recroom and found half the faction clustered around the main screen.

He tapped Natalia the Spy on the shoulder. "What's going on?"

Natalia goggled. "Are you kidding? Haven't you seen it happen yourself?"

"Let's just say my Downtime has been long and uninterrupted," Coster said icily. "Now players veto me when I'm picked."

"Oh. It's about Giger."

Coster wasn't all that familiar with Giger, within or without matches. The Gunner kept to himself, which Coster could respect, and as their in-game duties overlapped they rarely found themselves picked to play on the same team. "What about him?"

"His gun doesn't work," Kamen said simply, walking towards the huddle. "Just came out of a match with him."

Coster frowned. "Doesn't work?"

"Exactly what it sounds like. He sets it up on that little bipod, pours fire into the mobs, nothing happens."

"Same muzzle flash and collision particles," Natalia added, "but it's just a stream of bullets doing nothing."

"It's a plasma gun," Raya corrected. "I read his bio."

"The devs must have dropped an update," Kamen said sadly. "Undocumented changes. Screwed something up big time."

Natalia obligingly rewound the onscreen replay for Coster's benefit. Sure enough, standing on the top of a hill, the hulking form of Giger was blazing at the ever-advancing mobs. They were completely unfazed by the showy red streaks of light.

Normally a Gunner player was a devastating counter to a mob advance. Many a system would chug and struggle to render the wisps of blood and ash and ragdolling corpses when Giger brought his cannon to bear on a wave of fodder. It ate mobs and crapped out victory points.

There was something familiar, and disquieting, about the gritted teeth and steely fortitude of the in-game Giger. Features unchanging even though he was doing absolutely nothing to the encroaching horde.

Coster swore. "When did this happen?"

"The update dropped a couple of hours ago. And, uh, it's not just Giger," said Kamen. "It's all the v1.6 crowd, as far as we can tell."

"The usual," Raya stated. "They fixed something and in the process, broke something else. Big time."

Barely listening, Coster sidled across to another of the viewscreens and scrolled through the available replays until he found the character he was looking for.

"It's an obvious bug," Natalia agreed. "They'll try to get a fix out ASAP."

"Yeah, from what I hear Giger and the rest are laughing it off," said Kamen. "Sure, it ain't nice, but it'll be resolved soon."

Coster watched the replay of a man standing amidst a crowd, swinging a ludicrously gargantuan sword. He died a moment later, his killers unscathed, wearing a confident smirk right up until the end.

"You'd have to have some weird views about the game to take it personally—Hey, where did Coster go?"

***

"Evening, Giger."
"Yo. Coster, right?"

Giger's model was broad, topless, battle-scarred. Bald of head and long of beard, he was a foot taller than Coster, and while much of the Grenadier's bulk came from his bomb disposal-esque armor, the Gunner's was all muscle.

"Yeah, that's me. Sorry to hear about your bug."

"Eh, thanks, but it happens. Won't pretend I wasn't broken up about it but I'm not the only one."

"Regardless, it must have been a shock."

"Damn right it was. But you know what, the team still won. The first time I realized my gun wasn't working, we still went on to win." Giger smiled weakly. "Dunno whether that made it better or worse."

"What game mode was this?"

"Super Clash."

Coster made a face. Normally the appearance of Supers was an endgame event, a way for the dominant team to further ensure dominance. To add insult to injury, Supers entered the game at the expense of standard playable characters. A player would dump their character for a few minutes and enjoy a brief rampage as a Super, like the robotic Behemoth, or telekinetic Grandmaster: powerhouses that could rarely be stopped.

Super Clash, however, was a popular but tactically unsound mode where Supers were instantly available to both sides.

"I don't like Clash," Coster muttered. "Characters trying to fulfil their duties while avoiding enemy Supers. They run the show, make or break the game."

"Yeah. Tell me about it. You don't feel like you can do anything."

"Horde mode, now that's the real classic."

Giger grinned brightly. "You're only saying that because it's endless mobs."

"Guilty as charged. So. Funny question, have you seen Meraclus around?"

"No, sorry." Giger shrugged his enormous shoulders. "You try the canteen, or the recroom? Can't say I know the guy that well, those are the only places I ever see him."

"I'll keep my eyes open. I bet I'll meet you in the field soon, Giger."

"I hope so too, man. Later."

Heedless of Giger's suggestion, Coster continued down the corridor and tried the observation floor. A few people were gathered to watch the sights, but no Meraclus. Colored wisps of information danced on the horizon.

Coster realized he was thinking about this all wrong. He backed up, went all the way to the other side of the Downtime complex, defying ominous warning signs to reach the barren and deserted platform that overlooked the endless void of absent data.

Barren and deserted, that is, except for Meraclus, sat at the precipice.

"Meraclus?"

He didn't respond. He was staring at the abyss, his legs dangling.

The gray emptiness wouldn't be gray emptiness forever. If an update dropped and implemented more content, the resulting addition to the complex would crush Meraclus against the platform edge like so much discarded code.

Coster swallowed. "Meraclus, you might want to get away from there."

Meraclus turned, and finally banished his default expression with a forced, sour grin that hadn't been implemented by any programmer. "You're here to laugh too, huh?"

Coster blinked. "Laugh?"

"Everyone gets to poke fun at the big jerk that all the new players flock to because he's a scrub, and you can point and click to make things die and not much else, and now he can't even do that."

Coster moved in closer. "Hey, you're the backbone of the team, cut that out."

Meraclus rolled his glowing eyes and returned to staring at the void. "You don't know me at all."

Coster laid a hand on his shoulder and pulled him up.

"Bullshit. I know you're good at what you do, and the team needs that."

Meraclus looked dazed, defeated. He didn't resist as Coster maneuvered him away from the edge. "The team resents me, more like. Taking all the glory."

"No. The team loves to see you enter the fight. When you burst into action nobody thinks 'Wow, that asshole stole my kill.' They think 'Damn, I'm sure glad Meraclus was there, that could have been nasty.' It's what you're there for. When you pop your Apex, bam, the enemy is in trouble."

Apex abilities were the last and most powerful skills unlocked by characters as a match progressed, and Meraclus was no exception. Coster wasn't exaggerating: his own Bombardment may have had a wide area of effect, but Meraclus and his Enchanted Edge had been known to best entire enemy teams.

"They're happy to see me gone."

"No, because that ruins our own chances. But everyone is jealous of you if that's what you're saying. Who wouldn't be!"

"You're not jealous."

"I'm not—damn, Meraclus," Coster shook his head, "I know my own mind, and my mind is jealous as Hell. I'd be green with envy if I wasn't already blue for some reason. Everyone wants to be Meraclus, the Arcane Commando."

Meraclus said nothing.

"And I don't know if you noticed, but you're not the only one. All the v1.6 characters are affected. I was just talking to Giger about it."

Meraclus looked surprised. "How's Giger taking it?"

"As well as can be expected. Something must have gone really wrong, so you can bet your magic ass they'll rush to release a fix."

They stood and stared into the blankness. An absence of content, but who's to say it wouldn't soon be occupied?

"Thanks, Coster. I'm sorry I was a jerk."

"I've been killing people with an overpowered ability for months, so maybe I deserved it."

"I was still a jerk."

"Well, yeah. But I'm sure you can patch that out in the future."

***

CostersCommander
Newbie

Hi everyone! long time player, first time on the forum, really happy to be here
As you can probably tell hahhah I play a lot of grenadier so I am v glad you fixed the bombard bug so I could play him again, but in a

comp stomp last night me and a few other guys saw what mightve been a bug
we let the bots hit top tier (lol just for fun) and they spawned Behemoth, but we noticed something... the grenadiers Anti Armor shot worked on it

Turns out a behemoth goes down real fast w/out armor! foot, skirmisher, and the arc commando took it out in like ten seconds. this is obvs really cool but since p much all character abilities cant do anything to Supers, we wondered if it was a new glitch...
Just being nosy! keep up the good work

……… ……… ……… ……… ………

Drakeguy
Project Lead

Thank you for your query, we are glad to have you with us.
I can report that this feature is working as intended.

Supercollider
Alan Williamson

"This city is filled with hollowness."

The pig man let out a derisive snort, smoke wafting out of his flared nostrils.

"That's the most pretentious shit I ever heard, Nick." Nick swirled the cold coffee in his mug and forced down the gritty dregs. Unhindered by the pig man's sneer, he continued.

"The people I see on my shift—the pedestrians. It's like they have nowhere to go, nothing to do, they just wander like zombies. I look at them and I think to myself, if I swerved onto the sidewalk, would you even jump out of the way?"

"I'm sure some of them would," shrugged the pig man, taking another apathetic drag of his cigarette.

Nick removed a dwindling pouch of tobacco from his jacket pocket and danced a cigarette into existence between his fingers. He glanced at the pig man. Maybe it was unfair to think of him as a pig man, but his mannerisms were disgusting. A thin layer of grease clung to his face; the beads of sweat dribbling from his forehead formed oil slicks. He sagged on the inside.

"And what about the others?" asked Nick.

"Well, not everybody wants to jump, and not everybody needs to," said the pig man.

Nick quite liked pigs, just not this one.

***

On this well-worn route, the road wasn't potholed, just differently textured. Nick drove through here for convenience rather than the scenery: there wasn't a lot to see unless you were an admirer of nondescript concrete cubes with painted-on doors and windows. Most of the buildings here were abandoned, but not derelict. Some of them looked like they'd never been used at all.

When work was slow, Nick would park and watch the people pass by. He carried a small notebook with him for writing daily observations, self-indulgent philosophy and doggerel verse. That which used to provide inspiration now only brought stagnation. Were these people happy? Unhappy? Alive? Dead? He couldn't tell anymore. He used to be able to tell, or so he thought.

Now these pedestrians drifted aimlessly without even acknowledging each other. If not for the shopping bags and predictable clothing changes from businesspeople to late night revellers, he could have sworn they were all travelling in circles.

Today there was something different. A little kid in a red T-shirt and shorts was weaving up the sidewalk between the stoic giants. He was clutching a well-loved teddy bear, gesticulating wildly with it, talking to it, making exaggerated movements without bumping into anyone as only a child can. He looked like he was having a grand adventure. He was the only one. What must have been his parent was following behind, stony-faced in conversation.

Nick clicked his pen and flipped to a blank page in his dog-eared notebook. "One small particle, part of the crowd, somehow not colliding," he wrote. He could fix that later, he said to himself, but he knew deep down he never would. The more he analyzed his writing, the worse it seemed.

There was a knock on the window and Nick jolted out of his scribbling. A woman on the pavement waved his attention and he gestured for her to get into the cab. He cracked open the seal on the fresh packet of tobacco he'd bought earlier, but thought better of sparking up when the passenger shot him a glare.

"Take me to the train station."

He nodded, saying nothing as he tapped the meter and the numbers started to roll. The train station was miles away. He hoped his passenger didn't have a strict time limit. At least he'd get some decent earnings for it, especially since he figured she was a tourist and he could extend the journey artificially by meandering through some side streets. The trick was to learn the right combinations so you never doubled back on yourself and disoriented the customer. He did that quite a lot, for the challenge, to see how high a score he could rack up on the meter. He often got it wrong (once an irate passenger leapt out of the cab in frustration) but that was part of the thrill, and in a city this big you never ran out of chances. There was always another day. This game of deceit broke up the monotony of the evening, but lately he didn't have the enthusiasm to play the game.

Nick glanced in the rear-view mirror. His passenger was looking out the window, where generic beige boxes had parted to make way for doorless glass edifices. The skyscrapers had a pristine, pre-baked glaze. The workers walking past were unreflected in the glass, like vampires masquerading as human. In a concrete courtyard in front of an office block, skateboarders were leaping the staircases and grinding the ledges, laughing at a bemused security guard struggling to remove them from the premises. They wouldn't be satisfied until they had mastered every line.

The passenger's expression changed from ambivalence to that of bittersweet nostalgia. Her foundation strained around the eyes as she squinted at the skaters and their act of fleeting rebellion. Searching her eyes for an emotion, Nick suddenly realized his own eyes weren't on the road. He slammed hard on the brakes to avoid hitting the car in front. His passenger broke out of her thought and gave him that glare again, one he pretended not to notice. They reached the station and she left without a goodbye, but her face stayed with him. She looked like she'd lost something.

Back on the road, cars and bikes weaved endlessly through every road and junction—mechanical fireflies. Nick wondered how a bird's-eye view of the city would look: maybe like a computer's motherboard with visible electric pulses. The traffic lights were logic gates that let the vehicles pass, but there was no logic to this repetition. Electrons have no sense of self, and neither did the people in the cars. They were just energy without agency taking the path of least resistance.

***

"I remember in high school, we watched smoke move under a microscope. It's hard to think of anything more...fluid than smoke, right?"

"I guess," said the pig man. Nick didn't care about his ambivalence. At this point in the evening, he would have found talking to a wall therapeutic.

"So, when you look at smoke under the microscope, you see it's not smoke at all. It's actually made of these particles. They flicker like specks of ash. They're all jiggling around."

"Mmm, I thought smoke was fluid," the pig man snorted. Wisps of smoke rushed out of his nose and rippled across the table.

"Nah, it's an illusion." Nick reached for his pouch of tobacco, but inside were mere wisps of leaf. "I think it's called Brownian Motion. The smoke jiggles because other bits of smoke keep bumping into it, knocking them off course. Yet, all these collisions and it looks smooth when you're not looking through the microscope. It's a paradox!"

Despite Nick's renewed enthusiasm for high school chemistry, the pig man smoked and brooded undeterred. He never looked directly at Nick, preferring to focus on nothing at all. A stain on the wall, a moth by the light outdoors: anything caught his attention, yet nothing gained his interest.

"I'm sick of just being part of the smoke. I want to be more than just a collider."

The pig man's smoke belched on, liquid across the table, a solid wave crashing on Nick's skin. He took a deep drag and tapped his ash into the tray. A speck of burning paper drifted free and floated through the air, dissolving into vapor. A flickering dot of flame remained. One small particle, part of the crowd, somehow not colliding.

***

Taking the subway home from work was refreshing. Nick couldn't drive for pleasure anymore; he hadn't enjoyed driving for years. When he'd first taken the taxi job, nothing else was available. In those days, before his youthful optimism was replaced by the grinding cynicism of reality, he loved the idea of driving around town. Whenever your recreation becomes work and you don't find a new recreation to fill in the gap, it's easy to lose your passion for it. What used to be your escape from reality becomes the chain that binds you to it.

The air was stale down here, after the stink of daytime workers had penetrated every carriage and crevice. The other passengers seemed generated by cultural algorithms. Individuals— just like everybody else. Enough difference to differentiate them, but not enough to make a real difference.

A businesswoman on the train caught his eye. Her eyes were locked on her cell phone. Each tap was full of purpose. From his standing vantage point—after spending a long day moulded to his seat, he couldn't bear sitting on the subway—Nick tried to catch a glimpse of her screen. He didn't want her to know he was spying on her, so he strained his eyes without moving his neck. It wasn't very effective.

Nick withdrew his gaze. Probably another self-important nobody sending text messages to a friend that wouldn't remember them. He read once that billions of texts were sent every day: how many of those were just people correcting their own typos? How many megabytes of laughter that never actually happened out loud? Sometimes, he was really glad he had no one to listen to his jokes.

The woman shifted in her seat. Now Nick could see the screen more clearly. He couldn't help himself. He squinted at the text:

> "Without you, my lines have no punch.
> Every stroke of this keyboard is a crude hammering,
> Shouting into letters you'll never read.
> I'd read them to you,
> But you'd think I was a maniac or a fool."

Poetry. Not great—terrible even, barely coherent—yet somehow brilliant. His own work was rushed, disorganized thought stained with nicotine, coffee and cynicism. Sometimes it was about love, life or kids playing in the street, but often it wasn't about anything. He'd always thought he was writing for himself, but maybe he was just writing in the hope that one day someone would read it, like the woman on the train.

He thought about the boy and his bear, the passenger who longed to be free again, the lover trapped on a train. The train was too warm, he couldn't breathe. As the interminable ride went on, the layers of cynicism unraveled in his mind like a mummy's bandages, liberating previously muffled senses. His limbs loosened in their joints, his heart raced a little. Great adventures and failed rebellions. The train was too warm. He noticed the other passengers in the coach: a man sitting with his dog, stroking the terrier's head behind the ear while it wagged in approval. They both looked matted and tired. Was the man homeless? Was he lonely? The humanity crashed onto him in waves. Jesus Christ, this train was so hot.

Gasping for breath, sweat running down his forehead, he pushed off the train at the next stop. Out in the street, the first shadows of night were creeping out from under the buildings. Where was he?

Pen on paper, poetry punched into plastic. Every crude graffito became a declaration of nonconformity to him, every bumper sticker a bold personal statement. The individuality enveloped him: a thousand jittering, flickering particles colliding with his consciousness.

Everything was poetry. He fetched the half-empty tobacco pouch from his pocket, crafting a brief moment of calm between his fingers that swiftly faded into smoke. He needed to bring himself back down to Earth. He was sure to find a friend at the café, whether it was a comforting coffee or a meat-headed associate.

***

Custard oozed out of the pig man's doughnut as he stuffed it into his face, emulsified dollops clinging to his unshaven chin. He passed Nick a cigarette, translucent with grease. Nick placed it in his empty pouch to shield his jacket: he felt like it would melt right through his chest and taint his soul.

"What do you think you are, Nick? Some kind of fuckin' philosopher?"

Why did he ever befriend the pig man? What was he doing here?

"People like us aren't meant to think about this shit," continued the pig man, spitting flecks of half-masticated doughnut onto Nick's jacket and into his coffee mug. "People like us, we don't think. We just do. Get up, go to work, no staring into collide-o-scopes or fuckin' staring at people neither. What's wrong with that? Are you saying that's not good enough for you?"

Oink, oink, oink.

Nick wanted to collide his fist into the pig man's face, but instead, he said his goodbyes and left. He was thinking about great adventures and rebellions.

***

He stopped at the waterfront and got out of the taxi. He was surprised they'd bought his excuse about needing an extra shift, an unprecedented request.

He looked around at the architecture. He saw those oppressive glass towers devoid of personality and the concrete boxes, but now he noticed the street vendors and shop owners filling the gaps. This was the first time in years he'd felt autonomous. He lit the pig man's cigarette and tossed it into the front seat of the cab. It slowly sunk out of view as it melted through the fabric. It was a good day to quit.

"If you stand in one place while the world turns, you end up falling off its edge." He had read that somewhere. Maybe he had written it himself in a coffee-and-hate-stained notebook; maybe it was a line of terrible love poetry. Either way, it seemed illogical to complain about passivity and remain passive yourself. It was no longer enough for him to be a random collider in a cell. The monotonous predictability of life was more toxic than his nicotine addiction.

Suddenly from inside the taxi came a violent catharsis. The chassis burst outward as the fuel inside gasped for air. Glass shards rained onto the worn concrete, and then came the flames Nick had been yearning for. They flickered unpredictably. Nick smiled and watched them dance into the sky, which was now showing the first hints of day. He couldn't remember the last time he'd actually watched the sunrise. He breathed deeply, filling his lungs with a mix of cold dawn air and acrid smoke. He watched the smoke billow, moving as liquid, jittering with flecks of flame. As he turned and walked away, there were more collisions to be made, and he knew they wouldn't be random anymore.

Good Losers Are Pretty
Andrew Vanden Bossche

Pretty Monster smiled as much as her sprite would allow and patiently endured the applause. The panel had just started, and she wondered how much longer they were going to clap. More than likely there wouldn't be any questions for her. The ones with the answers to *Perfect Summer Storm Forever*, from frame data to character design (or at least, more answers than anyone else) were Tim Kawasaki and June Snow. The pixel people were there to look pretty (which Pretty Monster did well, though strangely) and be friendly, which she wasn't so good at in person. Captain Summerknife was, though. He jumped on the table, tore off his sunglasses, and shouted,

"SUMMERWAVE NEXT! YOU'RE THE REAL REVOLUTION!"

And then the crowd was cheering and clapping all over again, and he threw back his head and laughed while the sunlight streamed through his half-real pixel-flesh. Pretty Monster could never hear it without having to pretend she wasn't giggling. No one was a better crowd pleaser than the Captain, and even if the slow startup and pixel-thin range on his spinning piledriver made him the third worst character in the game, no crowd cheered louder than one watching him win with it.

As the crowd settled down, Pretty Monster picked up her phone and browsed the forums again. The results of the convention tournament were already up. Notorious low-tier master Little Hexes flew in from New York to come back from the loser's bracket and win grand finals with Captain Summerknife. There was an embedded video of Hexes (just a kid, barely older than the first game) posing in sync with the Captain. She scrolled down for the full results, and down there she found Lilliput, playing as Pretty Monster, coming in sixth.

She thought about checking if Lilliput had posted a match analysis on the forums yet. It made Pretty Monster happy to read them. Her fans and players were the clever and hopeless, finding silly things for her to laugh at and coming up with new tricks and tech to win the impossible game of playing with the worst character in *Perfect Summer Storm Forever*. She was nervous when she first started posting on the forums, but her fans were ecstatic: "A REAL LIVE VIDEOGAME?!?!?!?!??!" was the first response she ever got, and she put that post in her signature, partially because it made her laugh and partially because she liked the enthusiasm and partially because it was true: that's what she was. But right now the forums weren't enough to make her feel better, not even a little, and when she felt like this as she sometimes did she couldn't help but feel guilty she turned out like this, tormenting thousands of kids trying to win with a character as unplayably bad as she was.

The lights were dimmed and the panel was starting, but Pretty Monster was far away. All over the world she was losing. She was losing in American double elimination and Japanese 2v2 combination cup. She was losing to the infinite combos of Misty Mako, she was losing to the thousand stings of the Witch of Wicker Wood's softly falling stars, and she was losing to the high-low unblockable of Mr. Mikado's delayed overhead slash. Her life bar was hitting zero in the summer storm stage of Summer Knight Kite and the alien landscape of Kid Mars and her home stage of Midnight Lake. She lost in South America and in the USA and Europe and Japan. She lost on the latest re-release on PSN and XBLA and she lost on the arcade-perfect Dreamcast port, and she lost on the machines still humming in the corners of bowling alleys in the Midwest. She lost on the bootleg systems in Brazil and she lost on emulators all over the world. She'd been losing since she was playable in *Perfect Summer Storm,* but she'd been no Geese Howard when she was the boss of *Summer Storm 2.* She lost to scrubs still complaining about how cheap her throws and ground teleport were. She lost to noobs who couldn't even pull off a dragon punch. She lost to trolls exploiting Glorious Goodnight Girl's Time Shatter glitch. She lost to Daigo and she lost to Justin Wong and she lost to the kids down the street playing in their basements.

The imported issue of *Arcadia* she bought on the show floor had it all in mathematical fact: 3.5:6.5 loss/win ratio, according to that month's rankings. It was down from last month and up from the month before, and the number had been higher and the number had been lower, but pixel for pixel, no one in *Perfect Summer Storm Forever* was worse than Pretty Monster.

The crowd had settled down and Tim had begun explaining the history of *Summer Storm* and the quiet future of their company,

Believersoft. *Summer Storm* was the last big hit out of Believersoft before they got too small for the world, a last ditch attempt to save the company by throwing their coolest, weirdest, most reckless ideas together, and it worked long enough for them to survive. Not many games are like *Summer Storm*. Not many fighters were also mysteries. Not many fighters let you win by flirting. Pretty Monster liked hearing Tim talk about *Summer Storm,* even though she had already heard everything he had to say about it twice over. She enjoyed the dark, too. Big bright places weren't made for her. Her character profile was very specific, and what she did and didn't like was hard-coded into her:

Likes: Small places, water, cool evenings, books, night flowers, quiet times, easily frightened people.

Dislikes: Crowded places, urban sprawl, the scent of gasoline, bright lights, monster hunters.

  Pretty Monster was made by some rules, and what she thought and who she was, what she had done and would most likely do, were as fundamental to her as her walk speed and the active frames of her heavy punch. *Summer Storm* was a fighting game, but it was more than a fighting game, and there was more to Pretty Monster than Tim and June ever thought there would be. They hadn't planned on her being the worst character in the game. It wasn't the only thing they hadn't planned on.
  Pretty Monster and her pixel-brothers and pixel-sisters passed through the world like the spectral glow of light from a CRT. It wasn't so unusual; Nintendo made an add-on for the Famicom in the early eighties that made videogame characters more real. They thought it would be pretty good for marketing and it was, even if, like the games themselves, the characters never acted exactly how their designers wanted them to. Making something solid out of metaphor was hard, but Nintendo had good engineers. It worked well enough, just not the way they were expecting; Mario jumped away into the mountains to hunt turtles and pick mushrooms and was never heard from again. Now he's just another myth in the foothills of Kyoto, a hologram, a chimera, two steps out of step with the world, a forest spirit, a modern Youkai. Nintendo retired making pixel-children around the same time as the

Power Glove. Nowadays, as soon as a ROM is dumped online, someone hooks it up and out they pop, pixel ghosts who wander the world like they're really there, more or less.

Pretty Monster was pretty, of course, but it was hard to tell exactly what she looked like. Her shivering sprite shifted like a river of myths, a rainbow of blue serpents, green plants and orange beasts. They were talking about her now, and the lead artist June, strange June Snow, was talking about how much she loved drawing her. But it was in no small part due to how carried away they got that they didn't know what to do with what they ended up with. Pretty Monster didn't work like anyone else, changing shape and moving like a river of monsters, giving her a dangerous potential to screw up everything in the game, top to bottom, so Tim erred on the side of caution, nerfing her from the moment she was born. It was hard to think of ideas for what she could do without making her more broken than anyone else in the cast, whereas Mr. Mikado, with his cool black uniform and pockets full of white stones and curved daggers, was easy, half-copied wholesale from every other fighter around. He played like an eccentric Ryu and pros picked him up instantly. Everyone liked him, but no one liked him the best, except people who liked to win. No one who liked to win picked Pretty Monster. Those people were playing for something else, and Pretty Monster wished she knew what it was. People who liked Mr. Mikado played in the tournament. People who liked her came to these panels. It made her happy and also troubled her.

"Being worst is better than being second worst," Mr. Mikado told her once. "No one remember the one that's not even good at being bad."

Strong words from the second or third best in the game, but he was right. Sly and dangerous, the main character Mr. Mikado. June was telling the audience he was made with the image of "an untrustworthy person you can't stop yourself from liking," and while he was a bad hero and a bad person he was a good friend, and he was never wrong. Mr. Mikado was quick to point out that there was really no such thing as "the best," no objective way to determine if one character was better than another, and he was right about that too, even if it wasn't much comfort.

All the tier lists could say, all anyone could say, was who was winning the most, not why. Maybe not enough people were playing the low tiers. Misty Mako had no poor matchups, but she was the hardest character in the game to play correctly. The only competitive players to make it to big tournaments are ones who know what they're doing, and some of the best players don't use the best characters. The greats don't play the game, they play each other. One of the tops players in Japan, SuperGoose, wasn't just the top player in *Perfect Summer Storm Forever*, he was the top player in every fighting game. He picked his games based on what tournaments were paying and what his sponsors wanted him to do and he won every time because to him it wasn't the game that was the challenge.

It was all too complicated to predict, and the ones who made the game understood it least of all. Maybe if the active frames on Pretty Monster's Out of The Depths special move were longer, it would change everything, like if the hitstun on Mr. Mikado's jumping heavy punch was shorter, he wouldn't have an unblockable mix up and he wouldn't be the second or third best character in the game. Just like Mikado said, you never knew. They used to think he was the best by a mile. Then they thought he was mid-tier at best. Then they found his unblockable and he shot right back up again. Pretty Monster, on the other hand, was both the worst and hardest to play. They were related. If she was easier to play, she might be a bit higher. She knew it and at first she wished she was, if only because then maybe more people would play her and do better with her. Maybe she'd have more friends and wouldn't have to worry about being a burden on the ones she had.

Games don't always turn out the way you'd expect. Misty Mako wasn't supposed to have such an easy infinite loop. Pretty Monster was supposed to not be the worst character in the game. Captain Summerknife blogs about cosplay and social justice when he's not at tournaments; they didn't mean for that to happen, though it was in his nature to strike poses and fight for justice. Being bad for competitive play didn't matter to Captain Summerknife. He had only one dislike: INJUSTICE, in all caps. He was not as simple as he looked or acted. He knew, and still knows, it's better to be cool than bad. The people who play as Captain Summerknife are the showiest lot. Some of the best players in the scene play Captain Summerknife. Grapplers are crowd pleasers, and the Captain is a silly, quotable crowd-pleaser, fun to win with and begrudgingly fun to lose to.

But Pretty Monster couldn't help thinking about just how bad she was. The last Summer Storm game came out in 1999, and Believersoft was working on other things now. They put a cameo of her in *Red Winter*, and she liked that, but it wasn't the same as *Summer Storm*. Being an enemy in a single-player game was like doing a job. Being played by a person was like turning into a human being, or what she thought it must be like to be a human being. Pretty Monster asked June and Tim why she was the way she was and they said her guess was as good as theirs. "We made Pretty Monster with the image of someone shy who might also want to eat you," June was saying. They showed all the concept art of her and all the dialogue they wrote and the design document and everything they could find. Pretty Monster liked seeing it all again but didn't understand what they were trying to show her; all she wanted to know was why she was so bad. At this rate, she was never going to eat anyone.

June asked her to pose while she showed slides of Pretty Monster's concept art. June had gotten better at drawing since the last *Summer Storm*. She explained how she drew so small the animation team had to keep magnifying glasses around the studio to see the details of her designs. Tim explained how they came up with the moves and attacks based on the drawings:

"We initially thought the shape-shifting would make her really feel like a final boss, but when it came time to make her playable we really resisted the urge to make her less weird. We thought that would disappoint the fans, so we spent a lot of time thinking about how we could use all of her animations while still making her fit as one of the characters."

Pretty Monster thought this approach was a bit irresponsible. She didn't need to ask if this was the reason why she was so bad at their game, and it might have even been the reason Believersoft never made it big. Pretty Monster had over three times the animation frames of the other characters. That struck her as phenomenally inefficient, and it was: sprites cost dollars. She felt a little guilty about how much she had cost to produce, but June didn't, and Tim didn't, and the fans didn't.

It was time for the Q&A. The audience usually asked the same questions every time, but Pretty Monster decided to pay attention anyway.

"Who inspired you to make games?" asked a fan.

"Ray Bradbury inspired me to make games," said Tim.

"What do you hope to see in the next generation of gaming?" asked a journalist.

"I want more young people to make games, but I want them to make games not because of my games, but because of things they did as a kid, like catching bugs in the summer. I want to play a game about catching bugs in the summer with the girl I have a crush on, because that was something that happened to me. A game based on a game about catching bugs might be a fun game, but I'm getting older. It's not the sort of game I want to play anymore."

"Why did you make *Summer Storm*?" asked another fan.

"Because I wanted to make a game about catching bugs in the summer with the girl I had a crush on," he said.

To Pretty Monster, Tim Kawasaki felt just like the title screen of his game: calm and laconic, the sunlit rainstorm over a field of dry August grass. June, though, felt to Pretty Monster like the title screen of the game she had been lead designer on, *Midnight Lake*. *Midnight Lake* gave kids nightmares, though it never got the company in too much trouble because it was hard to explain exactly why it was so scary. If moms and dads went pale over *Mortal Kombat* it was because they understood something their kids didn't. When they tried watching *Midnight Lake* to understand why it was making their kids cry, it was because the kids understood something they didn't. There was no blood in *Midnight Lake*, but there were glitches and lights and a mystery that kids spent quarter after quarter on trying to solve. June's monsters seemed to not be completely trapped behind the screen, and she liked her heroine Misty Mako, poor doomed Misty Mako, so much she put her in *Summer Storm*. At the end of *Midnight Lake*, the monsters are the ones everyone loves the most. June Snow said that was why it was so scary, and why even though she is the most popular character, no one can quite forgive Misty Mako. June was funny too, which is why *Summer Storm* was such a pretty and bright and cheerful and hopeless game.

"From a gameplay perspective, what gave you the idea for Pretty Monster?" asked a fan. The question didn't surprise Pretty Monster. She was used to being talked about in the third person. Out of all the characters, she was by far the most curious. But she was surprised to see that the person asking was Lilliput, still holding the custom controller painted in Pretty Monster's colors that she won sixth place with. Lilliput knew Pretty Monster inside and out. She figured out nearly everything that she could do, and when she won and especially when she lost, someone would ask her if she'd do better with another character. And she would, probably. But in *Summer Storm*, she wouldn't play anyone but *Pretty Monster*. "I can't win without her. I think it might be hard to explain, but I'm better with her than any other character. It's the game I want to play," she'd say, though it didn't make sense to anyone but her.

"I wanted to take what I liked about *Midnight Lake* to *Summer Storm*," said June. "Tim does the gameplay and can tell you about it, but I wanted something very strange and unexpected; that's why Pretty Monster's normal moves are hard to read, and she can teleport and fly. I'm not very good at fighting games, but I wanted, for once, to animate a character who was as strange to play as she was to look at. My favorite thing about what Tim does is that he makes controlling the characters feel like you're becoming part of them. Pretty Monster's controls are hard, but they feel more natural to me. Maybe Tim can say something else?"

"I'm really happy if players feel the same way," said Tim. "I don't see my job as being as important as June's. She does the real creative work; it's my job to be true to that. Does that answer your question?"

"Not completely," said Lilliput.

"What's missing?" asked June.

"Why's she fun to play with?" asked Lilliput.

Tim thought about it. Finally, he said "I don't know if anyone would know the answer to that better than you. What do you think?"

Pretty Monster had read every forum post by Lilliput, the theories and the cancels and the bugs and the perfect combinations that let Pretty Monster do things that no other character could dream of, even if she couldn't do any of them very well.

"Pretty Monster makes me feel like I'm free," she said. Pretty Monster had never heard Lilliput say anything like that before.

"I just want to know how you did it. Was it an accident? A coincidence? Did you do it all on purpose?" Lilliput asked.

"Yes. It was all of that," said June. "Mostly though, we loved her. We loved all the characters. We didn't love her more, but we weren't afraid to let her be what she was meant to be. If you love what you do enough and you know how to do it, we believe things work out. Not everyone will agree, but I am happier than I've ever been."

Mr. Mikado looked at Pretty Monster smugly. His expression said "I told you so" even more than usual. Captain Summerknife was soaking in the sunshine and he was shining, and his little brother Summer Knight Kite was blushing nervously. Misty Mako looked like she was annoyed about being talked about as if she wasn't there, but Pretty Monster knew she was really happy, and for a moment Pretty Monster felt a little bad right then for all the humans in the audience who were never that honest with each other, who hurt each other when they hurt each other. She remembered Lilliput joking (though not joking) about being afraid of her dad. She thought about Tim's kids and if he was able to tell them what he was telling the audience about his games. Looking tired, three cosplayers dressed in each of her forms had propped themselves against the conference room wall. They were almost as much paper mache as people. They were sweating, but they were rapt.

"What do you think, Pretty Monster?" asked June, and she handed her the microphone.

She leaned forward. "I think it's fun to eat people and humans don't do it enough," she said.

The crowd gasped, and then they laughed.

Who We Are

Lana Polansky *is a Montreal-based writer, game critic, amateur game-maker and professional scowler whose rantings you can enjoy on Twitter @LanaTheGun. She has written for* Kill Screen, Billboard, The Wall Street Journal, Five Out of Ten, Gameranx, Medium Difficulty, re/Action, Paste Magazine *and* Bit Creature.

Brendan Keogh *is a writer, videogame critic, and academic from Melbourne Australia. He has written for* Edge, Unwinnable, *and others, and is the author of* Killing is Harmless: A Critical Reading of Spec Ops The Line. *He writes infrequently on his blog,* http://critdamage.blogspot.com, *and too frequently on Twitter @BRKeogh.*

Ashton Raze *is an author, videogame developer and journalist from the South West of England. He is a regular contributor to The Telegraph's videogame section, author of novel* Bright Lights & Glass Houses, *and his first game with Owl Cave,* Richard & Alice, *was released in 2012. Follow him on Twitter @ashtonraze.*

Denis Farr *is a German-born, Chicago-based critic interested in how games, queerness, and theater intersect. He has had work featured in* Kotaku, re/Action, Five Out of Ten, The Guardian, The Border House, *and many other places that have been wonderful enough to have him. You can find him on Twitter @aeazel.*

Maddy Myers *is a videogame critic and columnist for* Paste Magazine. *She has also written pieces about videogames for the* Boston Phoenix, re/Action, Gameranx, The Border House blog, *and* Kill Screen. *Read her blog at* metroidpolitan.com *and find her on Twitter @samusclone.*

Matt Riche *is a Visual Effects Artist born in St. John's, Newfoundland, Canada. He's been known to tinker with music and ever-unfinished indie game projects. Check out his music here* http://retsyn.bandcamp.com/ *and his VFX work here* www.matthewriche.com.

Ian Miles Cheong *is a games journalist, freelance writer, and editor-in-chief at* Gameranx. *He enjoys playing with his dog* Isengard *and reading all*

108

manner of science fiction novels in his spare time.

Rollin Bishop *is a professional writer/editor based out of NYC. You can follow his ramblings about videogames and the weird corners of the Internet over on Twitter at @rollinbishop.*

Dylan Sabin *is a games journalist, editor at* Side Questing, *board game enthusiast and tinker living in Green Bay, Wisconsin. He spends his time building his own worlds and playing Dota 2. Follow him on Twitter @DylanSabin.*

Alois Wittwer *is a videogame critic and a true friend until the end of all ends; he will muffle the wails of your frightened soul. You can follow him on Twitter @TB_Love and read his attempts to productively disrupt at mediafactory.org.au/alois-wittwer.*

Shelley Du *currently resides in Victoria, Australia and is fond of dystopian fiction and JRPGs with attacks with names that sound like novelty gum. You can follow her unfiltered thoughts on Twitter @BigShellEvent.*

Alan Williamson *is the editor-in-chief of videogame culture magazine* Five out of Ten. *He is a self-exiled Northern Irishman living in Oxford, England. You can find him on Twitter @AGBear and find out more about* Five out of Ten *here: http://fiveoutoftenmagazine.com.*

Andrew Vanden Bossche *is freelance writer who maintains the surreal videogame terror blog mammonmachine.com and the Twitter account @mammonmachine, which is a popular resource for anime puns and flirtation advice.*

Ryan Morning *is a freelance copyeditor who occasionally does writing of his own instead of messing around with everyone else's. He currently lives in Cumbria with his tarantula and his Steam account. You can reach him on Twitter @Edcrab_.*

Max Temkin *is a designer from Chicago, Il and maker of* Cards Against Humanity, Humans vs. Zombies, *and* Werewolf. *The Chicago Sun Times said that his business has "the sophistication of a lemonade stand."*

Follow him on Twitter @MaxTemkin and check out his blog, maxistentialism.com.

Made in the USA
San Bernardino, CA
27 February 2014